"Walk me to the door, Mallory," Jake said, offering his hand and pulling her up from the sofa.

The front hall was narrow and brightly lit with mock oil lamps along its length. Jake reached the door and flipped the light switches, throwing the area into darkness.

"Why did you turn out the lights?" she asked.

"Because I'm going to kiss you," he said, his voice quiet as he pulled her around the face him, "and it looks like an illusion of privacy is all we're going to get."

Moonlight slanted in through the panel of glass in the door, and she could see the outline of his face, his shoulders. When she lifted her face to his, she felt the warmth of his breath on her cheek. The scent of brandy mingled with something masculine and spicy, and she inhaled deeply.

He was going to kiss her. Finally. It seemed she'd waited all her life for this moment, and she did what she'd wanted to do all night long. Lifting her hands to his chest, she pushed aside his jacket and pressed her palms flat against his shirt. Her lips tingled with the notion of offering them to him, and her heart missed a beat as she imagined how good it would feel. . . .

WHAT ARE *LOVESWEPT* ROMANCES?

They are stories of true romance and touching emotion. We believe those two very important ingredients are constants in our highly sensual and very believable stories in the *LOVESWEPT* line. Our goal is to give you, the reader, stories of consistently high quality that may sometimes make you laugh, sometimes make you cry, but are always fresh and creative and contain many delightful surprises within their pages.

Most romance fans read an enormous number of books. Those they truly love, they keep. Others may be traded with friends and soon forgotten. We hope that each *LOVESWEPT* romance will be a treasure—a "keeper." We will always try to publish

LOVE STORIES YOU'LL NEVER FORGET
BY AUTHORS YOU'LL ALWAYS REMEMBER

The Editors

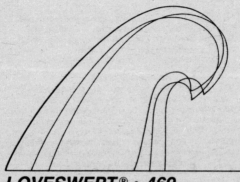

LOVESWEPT® • 469
Victoria Leigh
Secret Keeper

 BANTAM BOOKS
NEW YORK • TORONTO • LONDON • SYDNEY • AUCKLAND

SECRET KEEPER

A Bantam Book / May 1991

If you would be interested in receiving protective vinyl
covers for your Loveswept books, please write to this address
for information:

Loveswept
Bantam Books
P.O. Box 985
Hicksville, NY 11802

ISBN 0-553-44127-2

Published simultaneously in the United States and Canada

Bantam Books are published by Bantam Books, a division
of Bantam Doubleday Dell Publishing Group, Inc. Its trademark, consisting of the words "Bantam Books" and the
portrayal of a rooster, is Registered in U.S. Patent and
Trademark Office and in other countries. Marca Registrada.
Bantam Books, 666 Fifth Avenue, New York, New York
10103.

One

"Is there a problem, Carlson?"

Mallory asked the question without taking her eyes off her image in the mirror. There was something decidedly messy about the reflection, and she eyed it suspiciously, fairly certain she should be grateful it was a small mirror and didn't show anything below shoulder level. The face that looked back at her was equally wary, and she was forced to admit the assorted features added up to a somewhat disheveled whole.

Thick auburn hair fell in disarray about her shoulders, escaping whatever style they'd begun the day in and falling heavily in uncalculated disorder. As her slender fingers reached up to reorganize the errant waves, she exposed a streak of dirt that slashed across one cheek. Mallory rubbed it off with a tissue, blaming her less than impeccable appearance on Carlson's infernal haste.

Running a pinkie along the edge of her full lips, she corrected the smudge left by her lipstick and turned away from the mirror. "Carlson?" she asked again, drawing on her last reserves of patience as her nose caught a whiff of something being fried. She was famished, much too hungry to stand around and argue with the help about where they were going to sit. She crossed the foyer of the restaurant and elbowed her way to stand between Carlson and Vincent, making it three very hungry customers against one slightly alarmed maître d'.

"It seems they don't have a table for us," Carlson said mildly, a flicker of amusement crossing his features as he nodded toward the nearly empty room beyond the maître d's shoulder.

"You don't have a table?" Mallory's eyes narrowed on the increasingly discomfiting man, measuring his apparent determination to deny them entrance against her own considerable hunger.

It was no contest.

Sensing correctly that her two escorts were inclined to let her take the lead, Mallory stepped forward, not speaking until she was almost eyeball to eyeball with her adversary. "It appears you have several tables vacant," she said softly, taking care not to let her tongue trip over her temper. "Most of them, in fact. If I weren't so hungry, that in itself would make me wonder if it's worth eating here at all. Empty tables usually mean the food is mediocre . . . or worse."

"Thought you said the food here was good," Vincent grumbled from the sidelines.

Mallory shrugged off the implied error in judgment because the quality of the food wasn't the issue. Instead, she raised an eyebrow at the maître d's continued silence and tapped her foot on the carpeted floor.

The maître d' gulped, then squared his shoulders in a doomed attempt to regain control of the situation. "We have a certain . . . er, dress code—"

"And you think my friend isn't up to snuff?" she asked quietly, cocking her head toward the elder of the two men flanking her. She assumed the maître d' was talking about Vincent, a little scruffy in his nearly threadbare chambray shirt tucked into farmer-style bib overalls, and she mentally kicked herself for putting him in this embarrassing position. He hadn't wanted to come, insisting he was too grubby for dining out, but Mallory had dragged him along despite his protests.

Apparently, the maître d' agreed with him. Mallory began a slow boil inside, half wishing they'd chosen somewhere else to celebrate the near-completion of her new gallery, half ready to fight to the bitter end. If this had been a swanky club in the City—San Francisco—she would have understood the enforcement of a mini-mum dress code.

But this wasn't the City. It was Mill Valley, a small town north of San Francisco in Marin County. By virtue of the highly eclectic group of people living in the area, restaurants were usually open to whoever—or what-ever—wandered in. This one, the Mill Grill, was at the upper end of the scale in price and atmosphere. White-linen-covered tables were scattered under a high ceiling supported by rough-hewn beams that had been milled locally early in the century. An old-fashioned bar of polished redwood that graced one wall was equally ancient, although now it likely dispensed wine and designer water more frequently than hard liquor.

The Mill Grill had become a trendy dining spot long before Mallory had moved to the Bay Area. Obviously, it had now fallen from grace, she mused, although it still looked much as she remembered. But that wasn't the point, and she focused on the problem at hand. She recalled the last time she'd dined there, early last spring, when the Saturday shoppers and weekend jog-gers had comprised most of the clientele, people in sweatsuits vying with people in shorts and tank tops for the tables next to the windows.

Even so, she had to admit her own trio was a bit odd-looking.

Vincent, his arms folded across his chest, fixed her with his best I-told-you-so stare. She noticed that while he hadn't quite managed to brush all of the sawdust out of his hair, its salt-and-pepper color effectively camouflaged most of the tiny speckles. And with the day's growth of beard lending a grayish tone to his otherwise ruddy complexion, he managed to look hungry—very hungry indeed! It was a blessing, though, to note he looked less embarrassed than entertained by the skirmish.

Carlson, naturally, looked like he always did—elegantly casual in wool slacks and a cashmere sweater. The clothes did nothing to hide the extremely powerful body beneath, but they did help to make him look remarkably civilized—an appearance that could change if the situation demanded it. The mustache he sported was neatly trimmed, and he had made it a point to wash the paint from his hair before dressing. Of course he had, she thought. Carlson never went anywhere unprepared. And now, standing just behind her with his hands in his pockets, he took on the appearance of an interested observer.

For her own part, Mallory could only say with complete honesty that her lipstick was on straight. The rest of her didn't bear close analysis, although she was reasonably certain her jeans and sweater were appropriate to most any environment. She turned back to the maître d'.

"I really don't see why my friend's attire is considered inappropriate—"

"Jumping to conclusions, aren't you?" someone from behind her said.

Mallory later swore she felt the earth quake at the sound of the masculine voice, followed by a spark that shot up and down her spine in reaction to the husky drawl of the newcomer. She smothered a gasp at the sensation, arching her back in an involuntary response to the sensual sound of the voice. She prolonged turning to face the source, mostly because she didn't want to break the erotic spell. But he was an even bigger treat for her eyes.

He stood just a few feet away, leaning casually against a nearby doorjamb, submitting to her stare. She took in his expensive suit, noting the European cut and wondering if he was at all conscious of how broad his shoulders appeared under the jacket. Instinctively she knew his physique owed nothing to his tailor. His skin was dark, as much from the sun as his heritage, she guessed, her judgment based on the thick waves of almost black hair that fell neatly to his collar. He was tall, taller than the six-foot Carlson by a couple of inches, she calculated, but close to Carlson in age, about thirty-eight.

His eyes were gray. Not brown or green, but a smoke color that seemed to reach out and pull her across the room for a closer inspection. She felt herself sway forward, almost against her will. She would have succumbed, she knew, if it weren't for the laugh lines at the corners of his eyes that she noticed in the nick of time.

"Excuse me?" she asked. Her voice was a little ragged, but it was the best she could do for the moment.

"I said you were jumping to conclusions. There's not a thing wrong with your companions—either of them." Flexing his shoulders to push away from the doorway, he strode across the foyer until he was standing beside the flustered maître d'.

"Who are you?" she asked boldly, feeling a flush of color on her face as his eyes narrowed on her, excluding her companions. She stood her ground, patiently enduring his scrutiny because it gave her a chance to study him at the same time. It was an endless moment, though perhaps only a couple of seconds, before he answered her question.

"Jake Gallegher. I own this place."

"Jake Gallegher," she repeated, all her little nerve endings quivering once again at his husky drawl as she wondered where he'd picked up an Irish name with his Mediterranean coloring. Black Irish, perhaps.

He continued as though she hadn't interrupted. "What Perkins is trying to say is your own . . . er, attire is less than desirable." His gaze raked her from head to toe, lingering on the area below her knees as though to make a point.

"What!" The *nerve* of the man, she fumed, steadfastly refusing to believe this was actually happening to her. Never, *never*, had she been refused service . . . and certainly not because she was wearing jeans!

"Look at yourself," he suggested, a smile edging his lips. "Would *you* let someone with mud on their clothes sit in *your* dining room?"

"He's got a point, Mallory," Carlson said. "You *are* a little on the ragged side tonight."

Mallory was too busy staring down at her legs to respond to the sarcasm. No matter, she thought, blanching at the black goo that clung to her jeans. She could get even with Carlson anytime.

"I tripped in a pothole on my way inside," she said, irritated that she hadn't noticed the mud earlier, and incredibly embarrassed that she'd misconstrued the hesitation of the maître d' to seat them. Sighing at her own stupidity, she surveyed the damage. While her jeans were hopelessly filthy, the mud hadn't touched the knee-length lemon-yellow sweater she wore belted around her waist. "I guess I didn't realize I'd rolled in a mud bath."

"You should have said something," Carlson said, amusement clear in his voice. "But then, this wouldn't have happened if you'd let me park the car."

"Over my dead body," she muttered loudly enough for Carlson and the other men to hear. "You know how I feel about anyone driving my car."

"You still should have let me come with you," Carlson continued, familiar with the rhythm of this argument. "You know you're blind as a bat without your glasses."

"I can see perfectly well," she countered coolly, her eyes shooting stinging daggers at him.

"Sure you can," he said. "Except when you're driving, or at night. Once the sun goes down, you're a menace and you know it."

Mallory just smiled and reminded him that that was what the glasses were for. "If you hadn't been so afraid the restaurant was going to close before I got parked," she added, "we *all* could have fallen in the mud! Speaking of which." She turned to face Jake Gallegher with a belated sense of indignation. "Your parking lot is a disgrace. The potholes are deadly!"

"You have my apologies, of course," he murmured, his eyes lit with amusement at her counterattack. "As long as you're not otherwise hurt—"

"I'm not!" she said, wishing he'd quit looking at her as though he wanted to test for broken bones. It was enough that her spine was still quivering from the sneak attack of his incredibly sexy voice. She didn't need his eyes to go to work on the rest of her.

"It's on my list of things to do," he said, then added, "fixing the parking lot," as though he knew she was having trouble following the conversation. "It occurs to me, though, that walking alone at night is a pretty stupid thing to do."

"Because I'm a woman, you mean?" she asked softly, not minding at all that this battle was not of her choosing, because she'd seize any opportunity to linger with this new acquaintance. "For your information, Mill Valley is considered a safe town, and I won't have anyone tell me it's dangerous walking fifty feet by myself at night." Besides which, she added silently, Carlson had made sure she could hold her own against most would-be attackers, making a man's presence in case of an attack generally superfluous. But she didn't tell him that, because then the argument would be over.

"If you were my date, you wouldn't have that choice,"

Jake said, shooting a clearly disapproving glance at Carlson and Vincent. Vincent mumbled something about dating being more trouble than it was worth, and Carlson snickered at the older man's assessment. But neither jumped into the fray, and the restaurant owner shifted his gaze back to Mallory.

"But I'm *not* your date," she said evenly, wondering at the same time what it would be like to be escorted by this intriguing stranger. "I'm with these gentlemen and we want to eat."

"There's still the problem of the mud," he reminded her, and again critically scanned the mud-covered jeans.

"Then I guess if I can't eat like I am, I'll have to change," she murmured. Her teeth gently gnawed on her bottom lip as she considered what she was about to do.

The mischievous gleam shining in her eye should have warned Jake he'd pushed the wrong button. Carlson knew it. Vincent looked as though he had his suspicions.

But Jake Gallegher didn't know it.

Even when he saw her gather the folds of her sweater in her hands, he wasn't sure. When her fingers found the top button of her jeans, though, he knew.

Jake felt his breath catch in his throat, his chest swelling under almost intolerable pressure as he watched her toy with the copper-colored button. His gaze darted to her face, then back to her waist just in time to see her thumb push the button through the hole. Disbelief warred with the blatant evidence before his eyes, and then, as if she understood his need to breathe, she dropped the sweater, curtaining the movements of her fingers.

When he heard the faint sizzle of the zipper being released, he moved.

He closed the gap between them, standing so near to

her, nothing but a breath separated them. Quietly, evenly, he gave her another option. "There's a ladies' room down that hallway."

Mallory smiled, partly because he hadn't called her bluff, but mostly because standing this close, she could see the erratic pulse beating at his throat. Feeling reckless, she taunted him, carefully keeping her voice low so the exchange remained between the two of them. "You don't want to watch?"

"That's not what I said," he muttered, his breath touching her, his eyes holding her own. "I just don't want anyone else to watch. And I'll bet your boyfriend here isn't all that eager to have me look either."

"He's not my boyfriend," she said, dismissing Carlson without a single misgiving.

"Husband?" The thought hit Jake hard, making him want to lash out. A boyfriend he could work around. But a husband? A marriage . . . Well, there wasn't anything he could do about that.

Slowly, he registered the shake of her head. She wasn't married, at least not to either of the men she was with.

It was a step in the right direction.

"Not married," she murmured, and her smile broadened as she saw the brief flash of relief Jake couldn't hide. Neither was he married, she figured, basing her hunch equally on his reactions and her own intuition.

"Makes sense," he muttered. He clenched his fists at his sides to restrain himself from shaking some sense into her . . . because after he shook her, he knew he'd pull her close to feel her body against his. "No wonder he's letting you get away with a stunt like this!"

"Like what?" she asked innocently enough, knowing that now was a good time to back off. She didn't flirt often, and never so openly, but Jake Gallegher made her want to break the rules. "This sweater is perfectly decent—much longer than some of the skirts I own.

Why, taking off these jeans is no worse than stripping off a raincoat!"

"Stripping is certainly what it looked like to—"

"That's just your point of view," she interrupted, rising up on her toes to peek over Jake's shoulder at Carlson. Practice had taught her how to read the warnings beneath his amused expression, and she knew the time for modesty had arrived. Rocking back onto her heels, she decided to play it safe. "I'll finish this in the ladies if you're bothered."

Before she could take the first step, though, Jake snagged her wrist and held her still. He lowered his head until his lips were scant millimeters from her ear. "The next time you plan a striptease," he murmured, "warn me. I'll find us somewhere more private—where we can both enjoy it."

Jake heard her quiet gasp and released her, his hand faintly pulsing with the remembered heat of her skin against his.

It took Mallory ten seconds to peel the filthy jeans from her legs, but even with that record-breaking accomplishment, she returned to find the foyer nearly empty. Only Jake Gallegher remained. Without stopping to reconsider, she walked straight to him and held out the discarded jeans. She had to look up at him, because even at five and a half feet, she was considerably shorter than he.

"I think they're too wet and muddy to burn," he said, gingerly accepting the bundle with his fingertips.

"Perhaps you could put them through the dishwasher instead," she countered sweetly. Her nerves settled a little now that he wasn't looking at her quite so . . . well, intensely, she supposed.

"It's only industrial strength," Jake said, steadfastly avoiding looking down at her long, shapely legs.

"I doubt they'll ever come clean," she said, sighing her regret. "Too bad. They were my favorites."

Shifting his hold on the muddy bundle to catch an escaping leg before it could touch the carpet, he noticed a smudge of dried paint on the denim. "You paint in your favorite pants?"

"Jeans," she corrected him. "Men wear pants. Women wear slacks or jeans."

"Same difference. They both have two legs."

"The battle of the sexes reduced to an insignificant nuance," she said, her eyes sparkling at the swiftness of his response. "I'll bet you think the only difference between white wine and red is the price."

"There's more?" He grinned at the startled disbelief on her face and then, before she could find another tangent to chase, he nodded toward the dining room. "Vincent and Carlson are already seated. Why don't you wander in and find them. I'll . . . er, find something to do with these," he added, indicating the pants . . . or jeans. Whatever.

"Vincent and Carlson?" she asked, startled by his use of their names. "I was gone only a few seconds and you're buddies already!"

"Male bonding," he said with a grin. "Go eat before the cook shuts off the stove, Mallory."

She was halfway across the dining room before she realized it. Mallory . . . He'd said her name. She smiled, liking the feeling it gave her, then hurried over to the table. She was much too hungry to do the mental backtrack that would tell her exactly when he'd first learned it. It didn't matter, she knew, as long as he didn't forget.

"The food stinks." Vincent dropped his fork back onto the plate in disgust and reached for the bottle of house wine Carlson had ordered. He poured some into his glass, then offered it around the table before setting it back down.

Mallory put her nose at plate level and sniffed delicately, then with more enthusiasm. No odor assaulted her sense of smell, and she was unable to see why Vincent had made such a comment. "Mine doesn't stink," she said. "Perhaps you got a bad piece of meat."

Vincent harrumphed. "I don't mean it literally stinks. I mean it's badly prepared. Not to mention it's served without any sense of color or texture," he added, indicating the rather unappetizing lumps of meat swimming in a brownish-gray sauce.

"You're a carpenter, Vincent," she said, automatically chewing another bite. "Since when do you know so much about food?"

"I know a lot more than the chef," he replied evasively. "No wonder Jake declined your invitation to join us, Carlson. He probably eats down the street at that hamburger place. I'll bet those teenage cooks do a better job than the guy in the kitchen here."

"Enjoying your meal?"

Even the normally unruffled Carlson jumped at Jake's sudden appearance. Sharing a guilty look, the three diners silently voted. Once again it was left to Mallory to do the talking.

"Vincent says the food isn't up to the standard one would expect in such charming surroundings," she said glibly. "I personally think your chef is uninspired and probably a bit weary. It is rather late," she added, hoping the offered excuse would ease the blow.

It would have been all right if Jake hadn't looked at Vincent, his expression demanding confirmation. Vincent obliged, leaving Jake in no doubt as to his true judgment. "I said the food stinks. I wouldn't have said it if it wasn't true."

Jake didn't bother feigning surprise at Vincent's words. Like the holes in the parking lot, the food was another subject for reform. He hadn't gotten around to it yet, and was unsure of the best way to approach the problem. Firing the chef was one solution. Closing down the restaurant until he found another was also up for grabs, but he'd put off making the decision, mostly because in the three days since he'd taken over the place, he'd been too busy going through the books to give the kitchen staff much attention.

Besides, he thought, it couldn't possibly be as bad as Mallory and Vincent claimed. The few meals he'd eaten there had been tolerable, if not exactly exciting.

Mallory watched with interest as Jake leveled measuring stares at each of them. Then he did the unexpected. He pulled out the fourth chair—the one between her and Vincent—and joined them, sliding Vincent's plate across the table until it was in front of him. Unknowingly imitating Mallory, he bowed his head and cautiously sniffed the food.

"He says he didn't mean it that way," she said when he raised his head. "Vincent was commenting on the rather poor preparation, not an actual stench."

"I suppose I should be grateful for small favors," Jake muttered, then sighed in resignation as he picked up a clean fork and stabbed a piece of meat.

They all watched as he chewed, as though spellbound by his daring. When he finally swallowed, they awaited the verdict.

Jake reached for a glass of water and drank deeply before he pronounced judgment. "It stinks."

"Told you," Vincent said smugly, dabbing the corners of his mouth with the linen napkin. "Try some salad," he suggested. "It's amazing what they can do to destroy a few simple vegetables."

Jake didn't bother. One lesson was more than adequate. "I didn't realize things were this bad," he admitted, pushing the offending plate aside and reaching for Mallory's wineglass.

His eyebrows quirked as though he were asking permission. She really didn't think he'd stop if she said no, so she just smiled and watched as he turned the glass until his lips touched the smudge her lipstick had left on the rim. It was harder to keep up the smile then, what with his eyes telling her he'd done that on purpose and leaving her to wonder why the gesture felt so intimate.

"At least the wine is okay," he said, returning her glass to the precise spot he'd found it before raising his hand to signal the waiter. When no reassurance was forthcoming from the trio, he leveled a horrified stare at them.

"'Marginally palatable' expresses it better," Carlson said. "I wouldn't throw it out if there was nothing else to drink."

"What I can't understand is why you haven't done anything about it before now," Mallory said, drawing his gaze to her as she bravely tucked another bite of steak into her mouth. Poorly prepared or not, she was hungry. "With the odds of any restaurant's survival less than one in ten during the first year of operation, I'd think you might pay more attention to things like food and wine."

"No offense, I hope," Carlson added, throwing Mallory a warning glare. "It just seems you deserve better than you're getting from your chef, not to mention your manager."

"I don't have a manager." Jake thrust his fingers through his hair as he tried to remember how much easier life had been before he'd found himself owner of a falling-apart restaurant. "He quit when the last owner left."

"Tough break. I suppose that explains everything," Mallory said. Something inside of her was glad to hear Jake wasn't as inept as he appeared. "We don't usually run around critiquing restaurants," she continued, "but you seemed . . . open to comment?" She finished it as a question, mostly because she hoped a question would prompt Jake to talk more. The sound of his voice was quickly becoming something she liked a lot.

Jake studied her for a long moment, as though debating whether or not she was sincere in her sideways apology. In truth, he used the time to examine again the classic features of her face. There was nothing delicate about the high, almost exotic cheekbones, yet the porcelain tone of her skin lent an air of fragility to the otherwise strong face. A full, sensual mouth, thick dark eyebrows over eyes a fascinating shade of sherry, and a dimple at one corner of her lips were framed by a luxurious mane of auburn hair. The heavy waves tumbled halfway down her back, catching the muted lights of the room and reflecting them in a glorious display of changing color.

The waiter arrived, interrupting Jake's pleasurable scrutiny of her, and he got down to business. After checking with the others, he ordered simple omelets all around and a bottle of wine that Carlson insisted was palatable. Platters of half-finished steak were removed, although Mallory managed to sneak a last bite from hers.

"Thought you were too busy to join us," she teased Jake, fighting to keep the pleasure out of her voice. She put together an expression that was both innocent and curious and tried it out on him.

"This is business," he said, lifting an eyebrow at her expression. She seemed to be fighting a grin, and he tried to provoke it. "Sharing a meal with a table of critics is educational. I'm learning more here than I have since I first walked in the door."

"When was that?" Carlson asked.

"Three days ago." He made it sound like an eon as he shook his head in self-disparagement. "But what I can't understand is that the several times I've eaten here, the food wasn't spectacular, but it was certainly edible."

"It's an old chef's trick," Vincent said. "Make sure the boss gets the best so he won't complain. Then reduce the standards for the customers so you come in under budget. By the time the boss figures it out, it's generally too late. Works particularly well if the guy doesn't know the restaurant business."

Jake ignored the subtle probe, nodding slowly as he guessed the rest. "And the chef skims from the top of the budget, skipping out when things fall apart," he finished, catching on now that he had the basic plot in hand. "That certainly explains why business has fallen off in the last six months. I understand that was when the old chef moved on to a place in Napa." It also explained the discrepancies he'd found in the books, but he kept that to himself, feeling enough of a fool as it was. Instead, he fixed Vincent with a calculating stare. "What interests me is how you know so much about it."

Vincent shrugged. "I don't know so much. I'm a carpenter, have been for years. Helped build a restaurant once, though. You learn a lot, listening as you work, people treating you like you're part of the furniture, talking when they'd be better off keeping their mouths shut."

Jake wasn't satisfied with the answer, but it appeared to be the only one, so he backed off. The new bottle of wine arrived, and he indicated that Carlson should do the honors of tasting. "I've never had much of a taste for wine," he admitted. "Can't tell one from another."

"Obviously," Carlson murmured as he lifted the glass to his lips. He nodded his approval, and the waiter filled the other glasses.

"You don't seem to know much for a man who owns a restaurant," Mallory said, a challenging grin taking the edge off her words. She imagined she should temper her remarks, but there was something about Jake that made her feel daring.

Even so, she suspected she'd gone too far when Jake shifted his attention to her. His eyes were glinting, their gray depths reflecting a strange fire that obliterated all other thoughts from her mind. Instead, she found herself wondering how it would feel to have his hands caress the bare skin of her legs. They would be hot, she knew. Callused, not soft. Hot, hard . . . and demanding.

Unconsciously rubbing her legs together, she fought the image. It was too suggestive, too erotic. She ran her tongue along suddenly dry lips, and watched his eyes follow the movement, enjoying the almost physical weight of his gaze.

Turning in his seat and casually shielding his face from the other men by holding his wineglass near his cheek, Jake responded. Just for a second, just long enough to warn her that he could read her thoughts . . . and that he would someday make them real. With a gaze every bit as hot and wanting as her fantasy, he made her believe.

For one second he let her know he understood. Then, once she'd grasped the intent of his warning, she knew she could behave herself and hold her tongue, or take the consequences.

Yes, she knew what she should do. But she couldn't help wondering what it would be like to ignore his warning.

"I'll agree with Mallory, but more politely," Carlson said, unwittingly interrupting the sensual byplay. "I'd think problems like these would have been obvious if you had any experience in restaurant management."

"It's my first restaurant," Jake admitted, dragging his gaze from Mallory to look frankly at the two men. "This thing came up out of the blue, and now I'm stuck with a property that I'm not sure I want to keep."

"You have other business interests?" Carlson asked.

"A few." He left it at that, piquing Mallory's curiosity with the brevity of his reply. She had the impression he'd dabbled in several other businesses and wanted to ask him more. The thought of drawing his attention left her breathless, though, her body remembering the intensity of their last exchange.

But the challenge was there. . . .

"Now that you know about the crooked chef, what will you do about it?" she dared to ask.

He studied her purposely bland expression, then smiled, just a little, before replying.

"Fire him, I imagine."

"Probably not your wisest move," Vincent said. "Replacing him will take time, especially if you want someone really good."

"Keeping him around isn't doing business any good," Jake argued. "I'd rather close up the place and reopen when things are under control, if I keep it at all."

"And in the meantime you'll probably lose the rest of your staff. They can't afford to sit around and wait for you to get your kitchen in order."

"So you suggest I advertise for a replacement?" he asked, refraining from asking how much more Vincent had absorbed about the business as he was building shelves.

"A risky move," Vincent agreed. "If your current chef sees the ad, you'll be in the same position. Either way, things don't look terrific."

"And here I thought you were going to offer a solution."

"Sorry." Vincent shrugged, then leaned back so the waiter could serve him. "I'm just a carpenter."

"Sure you are." Jake let it go for the moment.

They fell silent as the waiter served the omelets, and Mallory watched as the three men dug into theirs. Suspicious of what the combination of steak and eggs would do to her overall cholesterol level, she only picked at hers, more involved with her thoughts than with the meal.

"*Now* what's wrong?" Jake asked, exasperation coloring his words. Between the holes in the parking lot, the lousy food, and equally lousy wine, he was beginning to fray around the edges. The last thing he needed was another critique.

"I'm full," Mallory said simply, a little surprised at the frustration in his voice. "I managed to eat most of my steak before you sent it back."

Jake couldn't stifle his sigh of relief. "I guess that's okay, then," he said, but he wondered how she'd managed to eat what he considered inedible. His gaze shifted to her gentle curves beneath her sweater, the creamy skin of her shoulders, and his mind skipped to another track. If they were alone, would she mind if he touched her there, in that shadowed hollow at the base of her throat? Would his fingers find a pulse beating erratically?

Or would it be his lips that set off the staccato rhythm?

Two

Mallory felt the heat of Jake's gaze and ignored it. Succumbing would have been devastating. She knew that, just as she knew a time would come when she'd have no choice. Jake Gallegher was a man like no other, the chemistry between them a powerful force. While caution had never been part of her inherent behavior, something inside her counseled it. For the moment, anyway.

Perhaps if she knew him better, it would make sense.

He didn't even know her last name, Jake mused. He knew there was less importance in a name than most people believed, but with a name, he could at least begin to develop some basic facts about her.

With a name, he could find an address. With an address, he could find her again.

"It's late."

Both Mallory and Jake were startled by Carlson's words. Given a test, neither could have testified accurately as to the subject of conversation over dinner, part two. Not that either had contributed much. Most of the burden had fallen to Carlson and Vincent, and they had spent considerable effort debating who was going to paint the bathroom ceiling in Mallory's art gallery, and which of them was better qualified to polish the mirrored walls abutting the staircase.

"How late?" Mallory asked. They'd only been there for a few minutes, it seemed.

"Late enough that we won't get a very early start tomorrow," Carlson said. "And at the rate Vincent works, we don't need any more handicaps."

"Time means nothing to an artist," Vincent said, grinning.

"You're not an artist. You're a carpenter. *Mallory's* the artist," Carlson pointed out.

"Then why does she hide her paintings in the laundry room?" Vincent asked.

"I have more taste than to display my work where everyone can see it," Mallory said. "My ego doesn't need constant stroking."

Carlson snorted, then drained his wine, avoiding her threatening gaze. Vincent, however, didn't know enough to take the hint.

"Well, she's just the right size for the bathroom ceiling," he said. "As long as we give her only one color to work with, I can't see where she can go wrong."

"I can paint circles around the two of you, so watch your mouths," she warned with mock seriousness.

"Circles you can probably do," Carlson said with a sly smile. "Anyone can follow a stencil."

"Then it's too bad we don't have a stencil for the bathroom ceiling," she said. "I'm obviously not qualified for higher achievements."

"I think she won that round," Vincent conceded. "I'll flip you for dinner. Loser paints the ceiling."

"Dinner's on me," Jake threw in, intrigued by their disparaging references to Mallory's artistic abilities. She took their razzing in stride, he was pleased to see. But from the mischievous glint in her eye, he knew she'd get even.

"Thank you," she murmured. She flashed him a

genuine smile of gratitude. "I'll look forward to coming back when you get things straightened out."

Vincent and Carlson added their thanks, and Vincent muttered something that sounded like "Lots of luck."

Jake stood with them, pulling out Mallory's chair, stalling for a moment alone with her. He didn't want much, just a few words, the chance to see her again . . . the opportunity to discover the taste of her mouth.

Mallory hesitated beside her chair, allowing Carlson and Vincent to file out of the dining room. She could feel Jake waiting behind her. Slowly, she turned, lifting her face until she could see him. He didn't speak, but his eyes gave him away. She took a chance.

"Shall I send you a notice for the opening?" she asked softly.

"Is it soon?" he breathed, knowing he couldn't wait long—*wouldn't* wait.

"Day after tomorrow." And she told him when and where it was, just in case the invitation didn't arrive in time.

"I'll be there." Day after tomorrow, he thought. An eternity. There had to be something more he could do. "Your name?"

"Bennett. I'm in the book, in Sausalito." She meandered through the scattered tables, and he followed her. In the foyer, Carlson and Vincent were pretending to look at various tourist brochures and matchbook covers.

"One more question," Jake said, stopping her. He had her name, almost had an address. Tomorrow he'd have more. "What are you opening?"

She grinned. "Now, *that's* a good question." But she didn't answer it.

"It's a gallery," Carlson said, clearly having eavesdropped on at least part of their conversation. "An *art* gallery."

"I thought you couldn't paint," Jake said, wondering

if he'd misinterpreted the banter about her painting ability.

"That's only an opinion," she said austerely. "But even I know better than to try to sell my own work. I leave it at home."

"Where it belongs," Carlson said, grinning at the evil glint in her warning glance.

"Anyway," Mallory continued to Jake, "you don't have to produce salable art to know what is good."

"She's right," Carlson said. "She does have the incredible knack of knowing what's going to sell and what won't."

"Seems like you catch a lot of flak for your talent . . . or lack of it," Jake said, enjoying Mallory's casual dismissal of the artist-bashing. After her cracks about the restaurant, he found little need to go easy on her himself. He smiled, enjoying the game as she shot him a look of mild disgust. Reaching under the reception desk, he pulled out a flashlight and tested the beam against the dark carpet.

"You're every bit as bad as they are," she said, overplaying her indignation so he'd know she was joking. "And just because some people don't like my paintings doesn't mean I can't paint."

"Nobody likes your paintings," Carlson said, leading the way out the door.

"And you'll be walking home if you're not careful," she grumbled, finding herself between Vincent and Jake in the procession to the car. Having two chaperons was becoming a tad cumbersome, and she was having serious thoughts about getting rid of them.

Vincent and Carlson piled into the car and sat quietly, as though pretending they weren't there. It made it worse, underscoring the knowledge that she wasn't alone with Jake. She looked up into his shadowed face, shrugged uncomfortably and slipped into the car. She said good-bye just before he closed her door for her. She thought he said something, too, but didn't catch the words. Fumbling for her glasses, she shoved them on, then put the car in gear.

Jake watched the taillights of her Jaguar disappear down the street and was heartened by two things.

One, he had her name.

Two, he had her pants.

Mallory stood in the doorway of the bathroom and watched as Vincent slapped a final coat of paint on the ceiling. "I still think dark blue would have been a unique touch there. White seems so ordinary."

"Dark blue is claustrophobic, particularly on the ceiling of a small room," Vincent said. "I'd think you'd know better, being an artist and all." Reaching up for a final stroke, he finished the job, then climbed down the short ladder.

"I guess I don't know much about decorating," she confessed, handing him the cup of coffee Carlson had brought from the corner shop.

"But I've seen your home," he said. "It's bright and airy—not a single blue ceiling in the place."

"That's Carlson's influence. He says I couldn't decorate a cave, even if all I had to work with were mammoth skins and dinosaur bones."

"Between that and your painting—"

"Enough with the artist jokes!" she begged. She didn't mean it, mostly because the teasing had become de rigueur among the trio. Over the month they'd spent getting the gallery into shape, the familiar jokes between herself and Carlson had extended to include Vincent, who rose to the occasion with a natural flair.

"No one who considers stripping in a restaurant should be ruffled by a little needling," Vincent said flatly.

Mallory granted him that point. Slouching down into a corner of a tarp-covered sofa, she toyed with her nearly empty coffee cup. "When did you see my work anyway? I never bring it into the shop."

"Of course you don't. You have more business sense than that." He dropped onto a matching sofa facing her. "Carlson showed me a couple of your pictures when I had dinner at the houseboat."

She sniffed. "Paintings, not pictures. Speaking of which, I need to get busy unloading those crates and get something up on the walls. I don't want to leave it all for tomorrow." Taking a satisfied look around the large room, she was pleased by the combination of the vaulted ceiling, the strategically placed display walls interspersed with full-length mirrored panels, and the dramatic curving staircase that led to a smaller viewing room upstairs.

Sighing in contentment, Mallory remembered her first shop, the one where she'd learned the intricacies of the gallery business. The trial and error period had been extensive, although not disheartening. Now, after two years of running a successful business, she was moving up. Her new gallery was the latest addition to a series of trendy shops located in an old warehouse in Mill Valley. It was a commercially attractive site, and one, she was confident, that would promote the works of her clients to the fullest extent possible.

And they opened tomorrow.

"I thought you were going to clean the mirrors before I got back," Carlson said as he entered the gallery.

"I called the janitorial service and suggested they include that with the rest of the cleanup," Mallory said, then grinned at the look of approval on Carlson's face. Then she asked him, because she couldn't stand not knowing, "Did you deliver it?"

"Deliver what?" he teased.

"The invitation!" she snapped, well aware he knew what she was asking about. "Did you see him?"

"Him" being Jake Gallegher. Mallory had hardly slept

the night before, what with her mind replaying with embarrassing clarity her outrageous behavior in the restaurant foyer, and wondering what Jake must be thinking about her and whether she'd ever see him again. Talk about regretting one's impulses!

"He wasn't there." Carlson crossed to the mahogany desk and made a note in the book that lay open on the blotter. "I left it with the chef."

"Now, that's a misnomer if ever I heard one," Vincent said with more than a trace of aspersion. "I sure hate to see a nice guy like Jake Gallegher lose his business because of incompetent help."

"And you could do better, I suppose?" Carlson plucked a paint-spattered cover off a nearby chair and sat facing them.

"Yes, I could," Vincent said. "It's what I used to be, a long time ago, before I got married. Before I ever got into this business." He swept his hand around the gallery, indicating his current occupation.

"How long ago?" Mallory asked, fascinated by his revelation. In the month she'd known him, Vincent had never mentioned anything related to a prior career, particularly one so different from carpentry.

"About twenty years," he said. Frowning over what were probably unpleasant memories, he told them the rest. "Grace—she was my wife—had a brother in the construction business. After we got married, she got it in her head that I'd never make any real money cooking. Cooking, that's what she called it. Couldn't appreciate the years of training, the skill that went into managing a kitchen. Anyway, she kept on harping about how her brother was making so much money and how he needed a partner he could trust."

Vincent cleared his throat, as if embarrassed by what he was about to say. "I loved her enough that all I wanted to do was please her. And I figured I could always come back to 'cooking' if the construction didn't work out.

Anyway, I quit my job and went into a partnership with her brother. We did okay, and I learned enough to get by."

"And you never missed being a chef?" Mallory asked.

"I missed it. But the longer I was in construction, the harder it was to get out. And then Grace's brother died, and I found out he'd mortgaged the business—twice! Well, in short, there was nothing left but to go bankrupt. And Grace, she couldn't understand how I could let that happen. She blamed me for everything—the lack of money, the loss of the business, even her brother's death."

"You're divorced?"

"She left me. Five years ago. And now I just take on small jobs like this, enough to get by but nothing too big."

"Which explains why you're slow as molasses," Carlson kidded Vincent.

"Maybe," Vincent said, smiling as he looked at the other man. "I never could see what rushing around got you that a little patience didn't."

"I don't understand why you didn't go back to, well, cooking," Mallory said, not knowing how else to put it.

He shrugged. "Doubt if I could get a decent job nowadays. I'm years behind all the new gadgets and the way they fix stuff now. What with all the diet foods—low cholesterol or high carbohydrate or nouvelle whatever—I don't think I'd have a chance."

The germ of an idea took root in that obscure corner of Mallory's mind where she occasionally hatched schemes and other mischief, but she gave no sign of it. It needed to grow, develop a little before she cornered Vincent. And Jake.

"I thought you'd like to have these back," the devil himself said. "You did say they were your favorites."

She jumped, rearing from the sofa as she assimilated Jake's abrupt presence. Automatically—and desperately, she glanced at a nearby wall mirror, then wished she hadn't. While her hair wasn't sticking straight up, it did manage to look as though she'd been flying with the flags over city hall in a stiff wind. At least the fuchsia ribbon was still there, she noticed gratefully, although she had to tug at the bow until it was centered again.

At last she turned to Jake, avoiding eye contact with him because her nerves were still jittery from his sudden appearance. Her gaze latched instead onto the jeans he was holding out to her. They were hers. She could tell by the familiar pattern of paint splotches.

"Thank you," she said, taking the soft denim into her hands. "I'm impressed. I thought they were beyond salvage." Her voice was gravelly and unsure, a perfect replication of the turmoil within. She hadn't realized seeing him again would hit her as hard as the first time, make her world spin backward and sending her heart racing along a course she hadn't traveled in years—and certainly never that fast!

"I bribed the laundry down the street," he said, moving to shake hands with Vincent and Carlson.

When he turned back to her, she told herself she was ready. A deep breath, and she tried it again, this time with more control. "You didn't have to come all this way to return them," she said, smiling so that he knew she was pleased he had.

"I thought you might need them for the opening," he said, his eyes sparkling with humor.

At the edge of her peripheral vision, she noticed Vincent practically dragging Carlson to the back of the gallery. Then she forgot them both, focusing her full attention on the man standing just inches away.

"I hope you won't be disappointed," she said, tossing the jeans onto the sofa, "if I turn up in something a little more . . . refined."

"I think I'll like whatever you wear," he said. His gaze drifted over her overalls and too-big work shirt. "But, somehow, refined isn't the first thing that occurs to me when I look at you," he murmured.

She blushed, recognizing his reference to her "strip-tease." Yes, refined was probably expecting a lot from his imagination. "I suppose demure and discreet would be stretching credibility a bit far too," she said, a little breathless from the intensity of his gaze. He could speed her heartbeat with only a look, she realized. Everything seemed to dim beyond the circle of privacy Jake created around them. They were alone, together, and nothing and no one else mattered.

"Other words come to mind when I look at you," he said, inching closer, touching her with his eyes, with his breath. "Words like *impetuous*. And *sexy*." He stared at the frantically beating pulse at her throat.

"You're not going to let me forget about last night, are you?" she asked, running the tip of her tongue over her lips.

"Probably not." His sudden grin broke the highly charged atmosphere. "I doubt if I'll ever forget a single thing about you, Mallory."

She gulped, then hurriedly changed the subject before she said anything impulsive. The temptation to say *You're the most wonderfully fascinating man I've ever met and I need, really* need *to get to know you* burned on her tongue, but discretion, for a change, won the round. Instead, she said, "Carlson delivered an invitation to you at the restaurant. You weren't there."

"The man at the laundry took a lot of bribing. Pay me back by having dinner with me tonight?"

"At the restaurant?" she asked before she could stop herself. Then she waited for what seemed an interminable minute, horrified that it had sounded as bad as she feared.

Jake breathed a sigh of relief, hoping she wouldn't notice it. She hadn't said no. The other part, about the restaurant, wasn't important. "No, not the restaurant. I thought we'd check out that new seafood place on the wharf."

"That's right down the street from our boat," she said, delighted at his suggestion. Her plan was coming together. All it would take now was a phone call—to cancel the reservation Jake had to make—and a bit of convincing that Vincent really wanted a midlife career change. She hoped he didn't prove too difficult. After all, it was for his own good!

"*Our* boat?" Jake repeated.

She smiled up at him, too engrossed with her own plans to worry about the sudden withdrawal she sensed in his voice. "Carlson and I have a houseboat in Sausalito just a few blocks from there."

"You live with Carlson?" Jake's brows drew together as he assimilated this unexpected piece of information. It didn't make sense, because she'd said Carlson wasn't her boyfriend. So why were they living together?

"That bothers you?" The buoyant mood his surprise arrival had engendered dipped to a depressing low, and Mallory wished she could take back that part about living with Carlson. She just didn't want to have to explain it now. Besides, it wasn't as though she could tell him the truth.

"It bothers me a little," he said brusquely. That wasn't an honest answer, so he changed it. "A lot," he said firmly, wondering why he didn't just walk away from it all. He had enough complications in his life, most of them business related, without inviting more. Getting involved with a woman who was living with another man was simply not on the list of things he wanted to do. So why didn't he just leave?

"Suppose I tell you Carlson doesn't interfere with my private life," she said. At least, not in the way you're thinking, she added silently.

"And that explains things?" he asked.

"He's not my lover." There, she'd said it. Mallory hoped that would be enough, because it was the truth.

Jake expelled the breath he'd been unconsciously holding. They weren't lovers. Well, that at least was something. Not all of it, but the most important part. He nodded, not trusting himself to speak. His nerves were raw, and he didn't want her to know how close his emotions had been to getting out of control.

When he didn't say anything, Mallory decided it was time to tell a fib. Not because she wanted to, but because it would head off the questions she couldn't answer. "He's my brother."

"Brother?"

"Half brother, technically." She hoped she sounded more positive than she felt. "Same father, different mom."

For several long moments Jake stared at her, dragging his gaze over the contours of her face, searching for any sign of deceit. There weren't any, he realized, and he wondered how he knew she was lying. The part about the brother was sheer fiction. But the other, about not being Carlson's lover, he believed.

Instinct, he told himself, and a lot of wishful thinking went into his conclusions. He hoped he was right. "Why don't I believe you?" he asked quietly, clasping his fingers around her arms gently, so that she understood he wasn't angry, just curious.

"Give up," she said. She had to concentrate on taking even breaths as she tried to ignore the heat of his hands.

He smiled, just a little, uncurling his fingers to stroke his palms up and down her arms, wishing her shirt were short-sleeved instead of long, imagining how her smooth skin would feel. "For now, I'll let you get away with it," he murmured. "But keep in mind I'm not a generous man. I don't share a woman with any man."

"I'm not asking you to," she said, frowning as she

realized the cover story she and Carlson had used for so long wasn't worth a damn anymore. It mattered, because she hated lying to Jake, even if there was a good reason for it. For the moment, though, it was enough that he believed there was nothing between her and Carlson. "In any case, I don't think the question of sharing is appropriate," she said, trying mentally to back up a few steps so she could catch her breath. "We're only going out to dinner."

"Are we?" he asked, not allowing the retreat she was seeking. There was much more between them than a simple dinner date, and he needed her to admit it.

"I mean, I hardly know you," she managed to whisper, spellbound by his gaze. It was like diving into a whirlpool, she mused, staring into his eyes. Floating, turning, swirling, deeper and deeper . . .

"We're going to change that," he said, then abruptly dropped his hands. They had company.

Carlson had finally eluded Vincent's grasp, and he sauntered back to the action in front. "Vincent found a mess under the sink," he said, grinning broadly as he inserted himself between Mallory and Jake. "He's found the leak but needs you to stick your finger in a pipe so he can fix it."

"Why don't you put *your* finger in it?" she asked. Trust Carlson to interrupt. It seemed like he was always in the way lately, she thought, and wondered how to divert his attention.

"Too fat." He fanned all ten fingers in front of her nose. "It's a little pipe, Mallory. And he's waiting."

"I don't think I want to watch this," Jake said. "I'll pick you up at seven?"

"Seven-thirty," she said automatically, managing not to meet his eyes, because she didn't want him to see the frustration in hers. Never mind, she thought, she would have tonight with him. And there was lots to be done before then, the least of which had something to do with a pipe and her finger. "Carlson will give you the address," she added, and headed toward the back room.

Leaving Carlson alone with Jake probably wasn't her wisest course of action, she realized. No telling what her roommate would say to him, although she was confident he'd at least pass on her address.

The rest . . . Well, she'd deal with that later. After she'd coerced Vincent into going along with her plan.

She wasn't forgetting the other plan she'd initiated earlier that morning, the one that had Vincent and Carlson volunteering to participate in a local eight-kilometer race in a few weeks time. The surprise was that neither of them had volunteered. Mallory had taken care of that part herself. They'd be speechless, she knew, when their pledge sheets arrived in the mail. And they'd have no choice, not at that late date. After all, it was for charity.

In the meantime, she needed to calculate how much she'd be willing to pledge for each kilometer. Quite a bit, she figured. It would be worth it to see the two of them sweat a little. Especially Carlson.

Three

Jake took his time walking down Issaquah Dock to the slip where Mallory's houseboat, *Tortuga*, was moored. It was toward the end, Carlson had said, the one with green shutters and a glass door etched with two beavers and a flamingo.

Two beavers and a flamingo? Jake shook his head in disbelief, as he had done at least a dozen times since he'd been given the directions. Sidestepping a black and white cat that was stretched out across the wooden slats of the dock, he slowed his pace. His surroundings almost demanded it. Tulips and bougainvillea sprang from many of the containers that lined the dock, and the profusion of plants surprised him as much as the houseboats themselves. He'd always thought of houseboats as transitory, single-level . . . well, tiny little houses on the water. He'd even managed to live in nearby Larkspur for five years without knowing he'd been wrong. Totally wrong.

These houseboats weren't transitory at all. In fact, the logistics of moving one challenged his sense of adventure. It could be done, he realized, but it wasn't as if you could just start up the engine and chug across the bay. Nor were many of them single-level. Most were two-storied, and a couple—it was easy to see, thanks to the abundance of picture windows—appeared to be a confusing series of raised and sunken levels that somehow joined to form a multistoried dwelling.

As for tiny, they were growing in size with each one he passed. He stopped at one point and estimated square footage, his calculations based on years of experience in constructing land-based buildings, and decided tiny was also wrong for many of the larger homes. They were at least two thousand square feet, he guessed, as much as a four-bedroom house in the suburbs.

He checked his watch and pressed on, finding the beaver and flamingo door in the next slip. A brass plate emblazoned *Tortuga* was screwed into the wall just beneath a set of green shutters. He punched the doorbell as he contemplated beavers and flamingos and turtles. Mallory opened the door seconds later.

"Why *Tortuga*?" he asked, his pleasure in seeing her again causing a definite rise in his pulse. She looked so good, he needed a moment to pull himself together.

She grinned. "You mean why do I have a boat named Turtle, or why do I have a boat named Turtle with beavers and a flamingo on the door?"

"Both."

"*Tortuga* was my dad's speedboat before he lost it in a hurricane a few years ago."

"He called it *Tortuga*?"

"*I* did," she said, inviting him in with a gesture. He followed, and she talked over her shoulder. "It was pretty slow for a speedboat."

"Considering your taste in cars, I suppose that fits," he said, referring to her Jaguar. "And the door with the beavers and flamingo?"

"A gift. At the time, it was pretty hard to say no." She shrugged, pausing to shut a window against the brisk evening wind. "Besides, it kind of grows on you." She turned then, her whole face smiling with the pleasure of having him so close.

Jake took a deep breath and thought about dragging her into his arms for the kiss he wanted so badly. She wouldn't mind, he knew, because it was in her eyes too, the urge to be close, to share tastes and textures. He didn't, though, because savoring the anticipation was part of what would make it so good when he finally did touch her, kiss her.

Instead, he brought up a point Carlson had mentioned earlier when he'd been giving directions. "Carlson says your driving has been known to reduce grown men to quivering masses of Jell-o."

"Carlson exaggerates," she said, hoping that was the worst of what Carlson had said. "Besides, he's just getting even because I never let him drive." She changed the subject, leading Jake past her display of petrified sand dollars and miscellaneous shells. "Have you ever been on a houseboat?"

"Never." He looked around the sumptuous room, as astounded by the size of it as he was by the fireplace at the far end. From the outside he wouldn't have guessed any of the houseboat's rooms was big enough to accommodate two small groupings of sofas and easy chairs, one set facing the fireplace, the other clustered in front of a large bay window. Ice-blue and mint-green fabrics lent a pleasantly misty feel to the room, with bold splashes of color contributing a comfortable warmth. At his back were two large Oriental panels, their size concealing whatever lay behind.

"The fireplace is a surprise," he said. "I never imagined finding one on a houseboat."

"It helps keep the dampness out, especially in winter," she said, leading him to one of the sofas by the window. "I can't imagine living without one myself. A fire is so—" She hesitated. She'd made the mistake of looking at him, and was now incapable of thinking of a single word to finish the sentence that wasn't entirely too suggestive. Adjectives like *seductive, stimulating,* and *arousing* were on the tip of her tongue, which, luckily, she bit.

"A fire is so . . . warm?" he suggested, obviously delighting in her confusion.

"That works!" She sighed gratefully. "We'll have one tonight if you like."

He undid the button of his suit coat and sat down, and she admired the brief flash of a white linen shirt before she realized she was staring. A swift glance at his face assured her he was still studying the room, so she rationed herself another quick peek.

He was dressed pretty much the same as the night before, a different suit but the same cut, his tie a subtle stripe instead of a paisley print. She liked how his hair curled lightly at the top of his collar, and she got a little carried away as she studied anew the intriguing angles of his face, the slight hint of a heavy beard, although he'd obviously shaved that evening. She looked hard at the laugh lines that creased outward from his eyes, the aristocratic angle of his nose . . . and all that looking made her want to touch.

But that, of course, was out of the question.

"Tonight?" Jake asked, surprised at her assumption they'd spend enough time there to make a fire worthwhile. Perhaps she was thinking about brandy in front of the fire later, after dinner. He warmed to the idea.

"Tonight what?" she mumbled.

"The fire," he said, grinning. Mallory was having a problem keeping her thoughts on one track, he noticed.

"I kind of hoped you wouldn't mind spending the evening here," she said, fiddling with the seam of the pillow she'd pulled onto her lap. "I arranged to have dinner served at eight. Do you mind?"

"Carlson cooks?"

"Carlson can't boil water," she said succinctly. "But

he's very talented at bringing home all sorts of takeout."

"We're having takeout?" With Carlson? This wasn't exactly the intimate evening he'd planned.

"Heavens no!" She laughed. "I'm having something special cooked right here. And as for Carlson, he had something else to do tonight." Or Mallory hoped he'd found something interesting to do. She'd shoved him out the door thirty minutes earlier with instructions not to return before midnight. "And I called the restaurant to cancel your booking, so I guess you're stuck."

She'd gone to a lot of trouble, Jake mused, noting the overflowing vases of fresh cut flowers that graced the room. The aromas of springtime combined with enticing hints of cinnamon and garlic that drifted from what he assumed was the direction of the kitchen, tantalizing his senses and alerting him to the prospect of a superb meal. A lot of trouble, he repeated silently. But perhaps this was Mallory's style. He settled against the cushions, resting his arms along the back of the sofa as he regarded her nervous fidgeting.

Increasingly skittish under his stare, Mallory bounced up and crossed to the drinks cabinet, not so much because she wanted a drink but because it was something to do. Checking Jake's preference, she poured them each a small measure of Scotch.

He took a glass from her with a murmured thank-you, managing to brush his fingers against hers in the transition. It was a small thing, the chance touching, but he found his attention centered on that tiny sensation. He knew it was something he would do again.

"Nice flowers," he said, veering onto a safe subject before he gave in to the impulse to drag her across the sofa and onto his lap.

"I think it's Carlson's way of apologizing for teasing me last night."

"And do you really think he's sorry?" Jake had his

doubts, particularly as neither Carlson nor Vincent had looked the least bit repentant earlier.

"Not at all," she said with a smile. "But when I mentioned how drab the house was looking without flowers, he took the hint quite gracefully." And because it seemed to be her day for ulterior motives, she had made a point of mentioning the lilacs she'd seen in the window of the flower shop down the street from the gallery. Peggy Markham owned that shop, and Mallory had been looking for ways to introduce her to Carlson for weeks. He hadn't said anything when he'd returned with the flowers, and Mallory knew better than to press him for information. As frustrating as that was, Carlson would go crazy if he even suspected she was matchmaking.

"Did it work?" Jake asked.

"Did what work?"

"The apology. Did it get him off the hook for teasing you?"

Mallory simply smiled, knowing better than to reveal her plans to anyone. "Let's just say he'll have to sweat some more before I'm satisfied."

"Something tells me it's probably not a good idea to get on the wrong side of you," Jake murmured, wondering if she was as merciless as her expression indicated.

She laughed. "I don't have a wrong side. But I do have a tendency to get even, particularly with unappreciative art critics."

"*Does* it bother you?" he asked. "I mean, having people bash your work?"

"Why do you ask?"

"Because I'm not sure if it's all a joke or not. And I think knowing that will tell me a lot about you." Jake thought he knew the answer; he could almost bet on her response. His instinct told him it *was* all a joke, that Mallory really couldn't paint and couldn't care less. But if he was wrong, if by some chance she was hurt by the barbs her close friends aimed at her, he wanted to know.

"I'm not a complex person," she said quietly, her eyes smiling. "I can't paint and I know it, and it doesn't bother me. My self-esteem doesn't suffer from the ribbing, and I give as good as I get. Friends are supposed to trust each other enough to do things like that."

"So if I make a crack about your paintings, it won't break your heart?"

"No, you won't break my heart that way." *No, not that way,* she repeated to herself. But there were other ways . . .

Jake nodded almost imperceptibly, his gaze catching the hint of disquiet that flashed across her face. A second later it was gone, and he couldn't be certain he'd seen anything at all. "Then I'll just have to hope we become friends."

"So you can take some more shots at my paintings?" she asked, feigning annoyance.

"There's that." The corner of his mouth curved up just a little as he anticipated the ramifications of getting to know Mallory.

"Just remember one thing," she said, using her most serious expression.

"What's that?"

"I *always* get even."

He grinned, mocking her threat with a total lack of concern.

"Don't say I didn't warn you." She held his gaze just long enough to show him she meant business, then lowered her eyelashes, guarding her thoughts from his probing stare.

Jake considered her veiled expression, wondering how long it had been since a woman had intrigued him so, wondering if he'd ever met anyone as fascinating as Mallory. She was easy to look at, not beautiful, but interesting. And elegant, he decided. The night before, standing in his restaurant in her muddy jeans and sweater, she'd managed to look classy.

Tonight she looked casually stylish. She was wearing another sweater, something soft and fuzzy with little sequins. It was a light pink, and the satiny skirt she wore with it was barely a half shade darker. The contrast of the knit and satin made him want to touch, but instead, he dug his fingers into the seat cushion.

Touching was out of the question because he knew he wouldn't stop with the enticing fabrics. They would merely be a beginning, leading him to explore what they covered. He knew he'd find silk there—soft, smooth, silky skin.

And her hair . . . It was falling down her back in endless waves, pulled away from her face with clips that looked entirely too delicate to hold back the heavy burden. It appeared darker tonight, different, and he realized the dusk of early evening had stolen its light. Later, he imagined, the flickering tongues of the fire would dance in her hair and make it come alive.

For now, it was her eyes that held his interest. Their rich mahogany depths literally sparkled with a glimmer of mystery. She had something up her sleeve, and he found himself catching her excitement. He tasted the last drops of his drink and leaned forward, placing the glass on the low coffee table. Then, just as he'd given up the battle against pulling Mallory into his arms, he heard muffled sounds from behind the Oriental panels, followed by a discreet cough.

"Dinner is served." Vincent, replete in chef's hat and a pink-striped apron that Jake unquestionably knew looked better on Mallory, folded the panels aside, revealing an elegantly set table.

"Love the apron, Vincent," Mallory teased. She ignored his annoyed huff as she enjoyed the astonishment on Jake's face.

"I thought he was a carpenter," he muttered out of the

side of his mouth before rising and extending a hand to her.

"I guess we'll know in a few minutes," she whispered back, then led the way across the room. It didn't occur to her to let her fingers slip from his grasp. It was only a short walk, she reasoned. Nothing to get excited about.

So why was her heart beating so fast?

Vincent had disappeared by the time they crossed the room, leaving them alone to admire the table, a dazzling sight beneath the low-hanging chandelier. Prisms reflected on the sparkling crystal and china, and the chandelier picked up the flickering flames of two candles, returning a reflection of a thousand flames. The prisms swayed almost imperceptibly, sympathetic to the faint movement of the boat and amplifying the effect of the candles.

It was as romantic a setting as she'd ever created, and Mallory wondered if Jake would think she was seducing him. That hadn't been her intention, she tried to convince herself. This was for Vincent's benefit, not her own.

"You notice he's not eating with us," Jake said, pointing to the two place settings. "Doesn't that worry you even a little?"

She sniffed the aromas coming from the kitchen and shook her head. "I'll eat anything that smells like that," she said.

He pulled out her chair and she sat, delighting in the scent of his faintly spicy aftershave as he leaned forward to push the chair back to the table. Food wasn't all that tempted her appetite that night, she mused, sighing as she reined in her galloping imagination. Lascivious thoughts were definitely inappropriate now, particularly when she hardly knew the man.

But it didn't stop her from wanting him, she thought,

lifting her head to find Jake staring at her from just inches away.

Jake read her thoughts in an instant, or hoped he did, and smiled slowly as he enjoyed the blush that rose to highlight her distraction. Then he released them both from the erotic moment and took his own seat at the other end of the table. Snapping the damask napkin open, he slid it onto his lap. "Last night Vincent denied knowing anything about cooking."

"He fibbed," she said, grinning up at Vincent as he placed the appetizer in front of her. "Didn't you, Vincent?"

"I look on it as evading the truth," he said gruffly. He served Jake before reaching into the ice bucket for the chilled wine. After pouring generous measures into the goblets, he abruptly left the room.

"Are you going to explain all this to me?" Jake asked.

"I believe it's endive with some sort of a lobster dressing," she said blithely, picking up her fork. "He wanted to stick to last night's menu to show you the difference in preparation, but we didn't have an appetizer then, so he's improvising."

"I meant—"

"I know what you meant," she interrupted, determined to forestall the explanations. "But we're not going to talk about it yet. Why don't you eat before it gets warm?"

"Is this supposed to soften me up for something?" he asked, then tried the salad. It was light and crisp and delicious, and he found himself neatly distracted from his own question.

"Probably," Mallory said. She was relieved he didn't expect more of an answer, and set about enjoying her own appetizer with much enthusiasm. She took another bite, chewing meditatively as she considered her plan. Proving to Jake that Vincent could cook was going to be a snap. The rest of it, getting Jake to hire Vincent, would depend upon how smart Jake was, because only a fool would pass up a chef that could produce food this good. Jake Gallegher didn't look like a fool.

Speaking of fools, she thought, it was about time she found out how he'd gotten into the restaurant business in the first place. Ignoring the direct route, she began her questions from an angle.

"What did you do before you bought the restaurant?"

"A little of everything," he said, finishing his salad and taking a sip of wine. "What did you do before the gallery?"

"This and that," she returned, grinning across the flickering candles at him. "Have you worked in this area before?"

"Marin County, you mean?"

"I guess so. I'd like to know that too. But I'm really curious about why you own a restaurant and don't know much about the business."

"I didn't exactly choose it," he said, leaning back as Vincent neatly exchanged empty salad plates for the entree. "A man owed me some money and let me have the restaurant in lieu of cash."

"You took his restaurant?"

"It was either that or a minor partnership in the string of health spas he has in Southern California."

"Seems like the spas would have been more profitable," she said. The exorbitant dues she paid at the gym she frequented were enough to make anyone rich. And since spas were just fancy gyms, she figured the rates were even higher.

"I wasn't interested in the spas, mostly because I didn't want to go into partnership with him. In the long run, the restaurant is a better investment. The land alone is worth a small fortune."

"Tell me about it!" She dipped her fork into the sauce that covered the medallions of beef, then took a bite. It was, in a word, terrific. She ate another piece of meat before adding, "The rent on my gallery is over fifty percent of total operating expenses."

Jake nodded, forking a bite of steak into his mouth. "How can you say this is what you ordered at the restaurant?" he asked incredulously. "It doesn't look, smell, *or* taste anything like last night's."

"I know." Vincent had slipped back into the room unnoticed, checking on their progress with a practiced eye.

"So what's the gimmick?" Jake asked him.

"No gimmick. I just used peppercorns and a light mustard sauce instead of drowning the meat in gravy as your cook had done. And the vegetables are fresh, not frozen," he added, indicating the brightly colored julienne carrots and purple onions. "It makes a difference," he tossed over his shoulder as he retreated to the kitchen.

Mallory knew enough about sales to keep her mouth shut and let the product sell itself. She let Jake eat for a while before returning to her questions. "I can understand how you ended up in the restaurant business, but that doesn't tell me anything about what you were doing before."

"I spent most of my working life in construction," he said easily, putting down his fork when a second helping didn't materialize. "But I got out of that a few years ago, mostly because I was tired of working around the clock."

Management, she guessed from his reference to long workdays. But that still didn't tell her enough. "And since then you've been sitting around waiting for the restaurant to drop into your lap?" she asked, knowing she was prying but unable to resist. This was Jake she was quizzing, a man she wanted to get to know, not just an acquaintance she'd never see again.

He lifted his wineglass and stared across the table at her, as though considering how little or how much to tell her. It made her more curious, primarily because most of the men she knew were quite open about their jobs and lives. She'd never minded listening, because it made up for her own reticence. Not that she minded talking about the gallery, but her private life was normally off limits.

Jake took a sip of the rich Burgundy, wishing for once that he could say whatever came to mind and not consider the consequences. Not for the first time in his life, he was involved in delicate negotiations regarding an investment scheme. Talking about such things required a great deal of tact and silence. If he said too much and it got repeated, things could fall apart very quickly. Not that he thought Mallory would broadcast it, but neither did he think he knew her well enough to take the risk. He settled for a partial truth—telling her what he'd done the previous month, more or less, and leaving out the current status.

"I'm involved in a new development in the East Bay," he said, naming a small town she'd heard about on the news a couple of times. "Last week I was finishing the package we're sending to prospective investors."

"You're looking for investors?" A tiny warning sounded in her head, the one that had to do with not trusting men who were more interested in her money than herself. Her sister had already been caught in that trap, and Mallory had learned by her example to be extra cautious. If Jake was looking for money, she didn't want him to look to her.

"Not really," he said, pushing his plate aside so he could rest his forearms on the table. "We've already had a lot of interest in the project, so it probably will just be a matter of weeding through the offers."

Mallory was relieved and intrigued at the same time. Perhaps this was one man who wouldn't care that her father was worth a small fortune. Jake's easy confidence spoke volumes about his success. He wasn't the kind of man to go chasing dreams. He wouldn't chase anything; he'd make it happen. She'd talk to Carlson about it, of course, and get him to find out exactly what kind of development Jake was involved in. It never hurt to be careful.

"Do you think I can afford Vincent?"

She looked up, startled out of her thoughts and back to the present. "I'd say you can't afford *not* to hire him."

"Which leaves us with nothing to talk about except—"

"The restaurant?" she said quickly.

"Uh-uh." Jake smiled as he shook his head. "It's your turn." He needed to know about her, what it was about her that made his heart beat with a rhythm that was familiar, yet exotically new. He could understand and deal with physical stimulation, had that been all of it. But there was more, something he couldn't define. Letting her talk might give him a clue.

"You want to know about the gallery?" Mallory asked, talking over a dry spot in her throat. What was it about the way he looked at her that made her totally conscious of his masculinity?

"I could listen to you talk all night," he said. "About the gallery, about your friends . . . or about you. Let's begin with you," he suggested. He sipped his wine, his gaze holding hers.

"Like what are my hobbies and pastimes?" she asked softly, threading her way through the maze of emotions that were surfacing under his warm regard.

"I was thinking along the lines of something more . . . intimate," he said, his voice dropping to a seductive murmur. "Tell me why I have trouble breathing when I look at you."

She flushed doubly, wondering what talking had to do with the hot look in his eyes. It was exciting, the way he spoke of intimacy. With a single word he lifted her above the realm of seductive banter and kicked her senses into a frenzy of uninhibited reactions. Her skin tingled, her fingertips itched with the need to feel his sun-darkened skin—especially his chest, where she knew she'd find soft black curls atop smooth, firm muscles.

If he touched her, she would melt. She knew this as surely as she knew the sensation of his hands on her body—*anywhere* on her body—would be devastatingly arousing.

Just thinking about it took her breath away.

"I've never slept with a man like you," she whispered, tilting her head as she studied him. It would be exciting and incredibly passionate between them, she knew. But did she dare experience lovemaking at that level, with all of her instincts screaming the warning that she'd never be satisfied again with another man?

"Excuse me?" Jake swallowed hard, gripping the arms of the chair in an attempt to keep from reaching for her. He hadn't expected such a frank response, not so soon. *I've never slept with a man like you.* Mallory had surprised him with her honest statement, surprised him because the women he'd known never gave that much of themselves away. There was a danger in sharing too much, too fast.

Apparently, she wasn't afraid.

Flustered, Mallory tried to correct the impression she'd given him. "I didn't mean to say—" Her words froze in her throat as she noticed his curiously pleased expression give way to a gentle smile.

"I know you didn't, honey," he said huskily. "But it was a nice thought. Just what did you mean, 'a man like me'?"

"I hardly know you," she breathed. She lifted her hand toward her glass, but retreated because she was shaking too badly to take a chance with the crystal. "You're a stranger. That's what I meant."

"Of course," he agreed easily, letting her get away with it for the moment. "And here I was, only talking about . . .

talking." But his eyes lied, and she knew Jake had already made his decision about what he wanted.

For that matter, so had she. That didn't mean, however, she'd give in to impulse. There was still the matter of his being a virtual stranger at the moment.

"I suppose we ought to be grateful that Vincent is in the next room," he teased before draining the last sip of wine from his glass.

"Considering we haven't had dessert, it's just as well."

"If you were in a hurry, you should have said something," Vincent snapped, suddenly appearing to remove their dinner plates.

Mallory and Jake exchanged startled glances, both wondering how Vincent had known the precise moment when their conversation had retreated from its provocative fast track, then they fixed their stares on the chef. Vincent just ignored them, fussing with brushing the bread crumbs from the linen cloth, then serving dessert and retiring to the kitchen.

Mallory waited until the door had shut behind him before leaning forward to whisper, "I'm one hundred percent certain I'll never be able to face him again!"

"You're embarrassed because he might have overheard you saying you want to go to bed with me?" Jake asked, dipping a spoon into the luscious swirl of chocolate and spice on his plate. As he lifted a portion of the feather-light souffle to his mouth, he inhaled a whiff of cinnamon before closing his lips over the rich treat.

"I didn't say that!"

He quirked an eyebrow at her and took another bite. The souffle was so rich and light, it was positively sinful. He justified the sin, though, making a mental note to tell Vincent to fix this only on special occasions. Like weekends.

"Eat your dessert," he suggested instead of arguing with her.

"I only said—"

"You said you'd never slept with a man like me. A man you didn't know," he added, rudely waving his fork in a lecturing manner. "Now, if you weren't interested in doing exactly that, why did you bring it up?"

Mallory decided not to answer. "Do you realize Vincent is listening to every word?" she said instead, trying hard to remember their twosome was really a three-some.

"Probably," Jake said. He finished his dessert and reached for the wine. He poured a measure for himself, then tipped the rest into Mallory's glass. "That means that if I casually mention to you that I'd like some coffee, he'll come through that door with a pot before you're finished eating."

"And if he doesn't?"

"Then he's more discreet than I give him credit for."

The door swung open, and Vincent sauntered over to the table with a silver coffeepot in one hand. "Waiters are discreet," he said stiffly, pouring a cup for each of them. "Chefs are temperamental."

"As long as they're competent, I can live with it," Jake said. "When can you start?"

"As soon as you get rid of that bumbling fool in your kitchen." Vincent set down the coffeepot and leaned against the sideboard, his arms crossed as he eyed the younger man warily.

"He's already gone." Jake sipped his coffee, returning Vincent's scrutiny. "I fired him this afternoon and put his assistant in charge until I found a replacement."

"Kind of got your order messed up, didn't you?" Vincent asked.

"Made sense to me," Jake replied. "He was doing more harm than good. There wasn't a chance in hell things could get any worse."

"Then I guess I could wander over there tomorrow," Vincent said, sounding for all the world as if he didn't care one way or the other.

Jake just grinned, knowing Vincent would undoubt-edly be there before the birds. The erstwhile carpenter's eyes were gleaming with anticipation, an excitement he couldn't hide. Jake could relax now, knowing that with Vincent's help the restaurant at least had a chance. There had been no real decision-making process about hiring Vincent. Rather, it was inevitable, just as getting close to Mallory was simply a matter of time and oppor-tunity.

"What about money?"

Both men turned to stare at Mallory, as if surprised she was still there.

"Vincent and I will discuss arrangements tomorrow," Jake said. "In the proper environment." Vincent agreed, shaking the hand Jake offered as he stood. Then the chef mumbled something about dishes and hot water and menial chores before disappearing through the kitchen door.

"Just checking," Mallory said, a little miffed at Jake's obvious resolve to cut her out of the discussion. "After all, this was all my idea."

"Brandy in front of the fire?" he suggested, firmly steering her away from the topic of Vincent's new job as he helped her from her chair.

"If you're sure you want to stay . . ." She took his hand and allowed him to lead her across the room.

"Don't pout Mallory." Gently pushing her toward the sofa, he said, "You've done your part very nicely and I thank you. The rest is between Vincent and me."

"I'm not being nosy," she protested, kicking off her shoes and curling up in one corner. "I just want to be sure he'll get a fair deal." Then, as Jake moved toward the fireplace, she exclaimed, "Don't light that!"

"Why?"

"Just a precaution," she said obliquely. "I'll let you know when it's safe."

Jake decided there was something about houseboats

and fireplaces that he wasn't aware of, so he didn't press the subject. Instead, he returned for a final word about his new chef.

"Vincent's old enough to take care of himself," he said, crossing to the drinks cabinet. He poured a stiff measure of brandy and took a long sip before splashing some in a glass for Mallory. Silently, he begged for her understanding. *Trust me,* he pleaded silently. Aloud, he added, "Pretend you know me well enough to believe I won't cheat your friend."

"But I *don't* know you."

"That's not the point." He settled beside her on the sofa and passed her the brandy. "There are a lot of things I know about you, even more that I don't. For example, you've asked me to take it on trust that Carlson isn't your lover."

"I told you, he's my brother!"

"Like hell," Jake muttered. Slamming his glass onto the coffee table with an indelicacy that should have broken it but didn't, he turned to face her. "If Carlson's your brother, I'm your maiden aunt!"

Four

"Sounds like a standoff to me," Vincent said.

Mallory sank into the cushions as Vincent strolled into the room, just about as embarrassed as a woman could be in the presence of her date and her carpenter. Chef, she corrected herself. And no longer hers. He was Jake's now.

Jake handled it better. "Excellent meal, Vincent. May I call you a cab?"

Vincent grinned at the heavy hint, and shook his head. "My truck is outside. Thanks, anyway."

Mallory waited until she heard the front door shut before she spoke. "If you still want a fire, the matches are on the shelf."

"You had to wait until Vincent left to start a fire?" he asked, shooting her a curious look over his shoulder as he walked toward the fireplace.

"Last time he was here, we all sat in front of the fire and toasted marshmallows. I didn't want to tempt him."

"Marshmallows?" Jake echoed hopefully, touching a match to the gas flame of the automatic starter. The fire kicked in, hungrily licking the carefully arranged logs.

"We're probably out of them," she mumbled, burying her nose in the brandy snifter. Why were the men in her life so fond of toasting marshmallows? she wondered. Carlson was addicted to them, and it hadn't been hard to encourage Vincent to get enthusiastic about holding fondue forks over the flaming logs. Now Jake was looking a bit wistful about the possibility of a sticky, gooey treat.

She felt as if her life were filled with boy scouts.

Jake waited a few minutes, letting the fire catch hold before turning off the gas jets and pulling the screen closed. Then he grabbed a couple of pillows from a nearby stack and used them to cushion his back against the brick hearth. It was comfortable there, stretched out in front of the fire. He reached for the brandy he'd left on the coffee table, his glance taking in Mallory's reaction.

She looked as though she couldn't decide whether or not to join him.

"Why don't you just stay there?" he suggested, his voice deliberately soft and comforting.

Mallory shook her head at the confusing input. His body language was open, inviting her to lie beside him and share the warmth of the fire . . . his fire. But his words told her a different story.

"I don't understand," she said, because she didn't . . . and because she wanted to ignore his sensible advise to stay away and respond instead to his silent invitation.

"I like looking at you," he said softly. "Almost as much as I like touching you. We're alone now, Mallory. No Vincent. No Carlson. Just you and me and the fire."

"And I still don't know you," she whispered, hypnotized by the smoky depths of his eyes.

"Which is why I'm down here and you're up there," he said. "Talk to me about the gallery."

He wanted her to know him, she thought. It was obvious, simple. Just as he wanted to know her.

So she told him. Abut the gallery, about how she'd

struggled to paint, only to find her real ability was in recognizing talent rather than displaying any personal genius. She talked about the artists she represented in her gallery, and her excitement over the new one.

She loved her work, and told him as much. With her hands and eyes she accented her simple explanations.

Jake watched, listening absently as he probed her soul. Mallory was dedicated, totally absorbed by her work. He tried to imagine the strength it must have taken to sublimate her own desire to paint against her true talent in promoting the artistic achievements of others.

She didn't resent it, he realized. Her own failure to set the art world on fire was merely a step she'd taken in the evolution of what she was now. She was content with her life, excited by her profession, and totally unaware of the seductive quality of her voice.

How could she know? he wondered. If she had any idea of how her voice was lashing against his self-control, she didn't show it. She spoke as if she didn't realize her tone was melting his restraints, replacing it with a desire so bold and fundamental, he barely recognized it.

The more she spoke, the more he wanted her.

The more he learned about her, the more he wanted to know. That was what kept him where he was, by the fire. The need to know more.

She was nearly thirty, she revealed, and he was pleased because he'd thought she was younger and eight years was enough of a gap between them.

She considered herself a medium, she said matter-of-factly, and he laughed because he thought she meant something occult. She laughed with him, then explained she was a medium tall, medium pretty woman with medium ambition. He agreed she was a woman and knew there was nothing medium about her at all.

The flow of words eventually shifted from her mouth

to his. One moment Mallory was describing in exacting detail the newest work by a favorite client, then somehow, Jake found himself talking about his day at the restaurant.

"The potholes are filled, and I'm going to have better lighting installed."

"That takes care of the outside," she said, surprised when she felt a pang of regret about the potholes. After all, without those grubby traps, she might have never met Jake. "Is hiring Vincent going to solve your problems on the inside?"

"I guess we'll have to see. But I'm more interested in knowing how you knew Vincent was good. *That* good, I mean. You admitted you discovered only today that he might know his way around a kitchen, so you couldn't possibly have had a chance for another demonstration."

"I guess I assumed it," she said. "If Vincent says he was once a chef, then I have to believe he was good at it. He's a friend," she added, as though that solved the matter.

"Which means he can do no wrong?"

"Which means he deserved a chance," she corrected him, smiling with the slightest hint of a challenge. "And after that meal last night, I figured *anything* would compare favorably."

"There's that," Jake said, returning her smile. "But now that I've hired Vincent away from you, won't that put a lot of work onto Carlson—what with the gallery and all."

"The gallery is finished," she said without concern. "There are a few things around the houseboat that Vincent is going to take care of next, but I think we can work around his schedule."

"And Carlson won't mind?"

"What's that got to do with anything?" she asked, knowing perfectly well that Jake was heading back to the subject of Carlson and the houseboat and Mallory and how they all fit together.

"I'd just hate to get on his bad side," Jake said. "He's built kind of hard and tough. I suspect he knows how to take care of himself—and anyone who gets in his way."

Mallory hid her grin with difficulty, not wanting to let Jake know how right he was. Carlson would be amused when she told him, but she needed to divert Jake's attention.

"I'd think with a new restaurant you'd be less worried about Carlson and me and more inclined to solve your own problems." She regarded him steadily over the rim of her brandy snifter. "And from what I've seen, you've got a handful."

"I make it a point to quit work early enough to enjoy the fruits of my labors," he said softly, toying with his own glass as he considered moving to the sofa.

"Not to mention meddle in my affairs." She meant to tease him a little about his preoccupation with Carlson, but realized as soon as the words were out that he wasn't ready to be teased.

"Affair? Is that what you call it?"

"An expression," she said, the color rising in her face as she searched for a graceful exit from a subject she should never have touched.

"A revealing one." The laughter was gone from her eyes, Jake noticed, and he knew their expression reflected his own. They weren't playing games here, and if Mallory wanted to taunt him with the possibility that Carlson was her lover, then he didn't plan on sticking around.

"I told you he's not my lover," she said evenly.

"Who's not your lover, Mallory?" Carlson asked from the doorway.

The crackling of the fire was the only sound in the room. Mallory burrowed farther into the sofa, wishing her tongue were less limber and her brain quicker to control it. She didn't dare turn to face Carlson, yet couldn't bring herself to focus on Jake.

This was, as some would phrase it, an awkward moment.

"I believe she was referring to you," Jake finally said.

"Oh?" Tossing his raincoat over the back of a chair, Carlson crossed the room and served himself a measure of brandy. Holding the bottle up, he nodded to Jake. "More?"

Jake rolled to his feet, the easy motion snapping Mallory out of her stunned reverie. As the two men walked toward each other, she crossed her fingers that neither would do anything stupid. Standing face-to-face, they only saluted each other with the crystal snifters, then sipped the potent liquor.

"She's right, you know," Carlson said, his glance flickering to where Mallory peered at them over the back of the sofa. "We're not lovers. Never have been."

"I believed her the first time she told me," Jake said, surprising them both. "I just can't figure out what the relationship between you is."

"You don't think she's my half sister?" Carlson asked, a grin tugging at the corner of his mouth.

"Not for a minute."

"Didn't think you would," Carlson said lightly, but didn't offer anything more as he turned away.

Jake followed him back to the circle of light where Mallory was gnawing at her knuckles as she watched the two men. He didn't press Carlson for another answer because it didn't seem to matter anymore. He knew everything important already.

He knew he wanted Mallory more than any woman he'd met.

"I thought you were staying away until midnight," she finally said to Carlson, a grimace of irritation crossing her face as he settled onto the other end of the sofa.

"It's nearly one," he pointed out. "Dinner was a success?"

"Absolutely," Jake said. He set his glass on the coffee table and turned to Mallory. "And it's time for me to be going. Walk me to the door, Mallory?"

He offered his hand and pulled her up from the sofa, keeping his fingers wrapped around hers even as he shook hands with Carlson.

The front hall was narrow and brightly lit with mock oil lamps along its length. Jake reached the door and flipped the light switches there, plunging the area into darkness.

"Why did you turn out the lights?" she asked.

"Because I'm going to kiss you," he said, his voice a whisper as he pulled her around to face him, "and it looks like an illusion of privacy is all we're going to get."

Moonlight slanted in through the panel of glass in the door, and she could see the outline of his face, his shoulders. When she lifted her face to his, she could feel the warmth of his breath on her cheek. Scents of brandy mingled with something masculine and spicy, and she inhaled deeply.

He was going to kiss her. Finally. It seemed she'd waited her entire life for this moment, and she did what she'd wanted to do all night. Lifting her hands to his chest, she pushed aside his jacket and pressed her palms flat against his shirt.

Jake's heart thudded beneath her fingers, strong and a little erratic, and she enjoyed the way it pulsed through her hands . . . the way it ignited a matching rhythm deep inside of her.

His hands rested lightly on her hips, and she felt the tiniest pressure urging her to take the final step. He didn't pull her close, but persuaded her, making it her decision. He wanted more than her hands on his chest, she understood, much more. Her lips tingled with the notion of offering them to his mouth, and her heart missed a beat as she imagined how good it would feel.

Because the excitement was almost too much, she stalled. "I'm glad you came," she said. She knew it would be only a few hours before she saw him again, but wished she didn't have to say good-bye to him because tomorrow seemed so terribly far away.

"Good," he murmured huskily, just a split second before he took the decision away from her. A slight movement of his wrists and she was with him, against him, her hands reaching for his shoulders as he pulled her into his body and took her mouth with his.

It was shattering, the sensations so intense, she couldn't separate one from the next. Her mouth opened to the hard thrust of his tongue as her breasts were crushed against his chest. She knew when he pushed her against the cool wall, when his hands left her hips to slip beneath her sweater, but she didn't think about it.

It just happened.

His hands were hard, controlled, as they explored her. She quivered as they slid firmly across her rib cage, trembled as his fingers caressed her heated skin and encountered the lace of her bra. He didn't touch the hardened nipples beneath the delicate fabric, but lingered for a moment at the soft valley between her breasts, stroking her with his knuckles before falling away. His mouth swallowed her cry of frustration, and he gentled her for a long moment with deep, drugging kisses.

Then, without warning, he drew her tongue into his mouth, sucking hard as he lowered his hands to the swell of her bottom. He brought her to his heat, shared with her the intimate knowledge of his arousal.

It was all or nothing. Mallory tightened her grip around his neck, silently begging, knowing only what was right.

When he set her away from him, the raging need he'd

built in her was out of control. She whimpered, and he lowered his mouth to hush her cry. Pulling her back to his warmth, he closed his arms around her and shared his own tremors of passion.

She felt the calming strokes on her hair, the embrace that was suddenly comforting and warm, a cuddling warmth that cooled a desire she'd never imagined.

"Why didn't—" she finally tried to ask, but found her mouth covered with his before she could finish.

He drew his tongue along her bottom lip, then slanted his mouth across hers for another kiss. She learned his taste, daring to push her tongue into his mouth, an exploration that was excitingly different from any kiss she'd ever experienced.

When she again reached the point where she had to have more, he answered her question, his mouth brushing hers with the words she didn't want to hear. "Not tonight, Mallory. Not here."

"The houseboat?" Did he think Carlson would listen in?

"The hallway," he countered, smiling wickedly at her gasp of outrage. "And some privacy would be nice too." Then he added in a voice that was low and sexy and sent chills up her spine, "I love those little noises you make. I don't want anyone else to hear them."

He ignored her second gasp and twisted the handle on the door. Pausing in the open doorway, he turned and cupped her face with his hands, then kissed her brow before moving back, away from her. "I'll see you at the opening."

"About Carlson . . ." she began.

"What about him?"

"Can you trust me on that for a while?" she asked in a low voice. "There's really nothing I can say besides what you already know."

Trust. Jake thought about his ex-wife and how stupid

he'd been to trust her when all she'd wanted was his wealth.

He considered Mallory's Jaguar and the sumptuous houseboat and the gallery, and figured she could take care of herself as far as the money thing was concerned.

"All right," he said, giving her the benefit of the doubt because he was already in too deep to deny what he most wanted. "I'll see you at the opening," he said again, resisting moving toward her again. He'd touch her if he did that, and then, maybe, he wouldn't be able to go away.

"I'll see you tomorrow," he promised. "At the opening."

"I'll be there," she breathed, unsteady on her feet because he was leaving and taking her balance with him.

He grinned. Of course she'd be there. And afterward . . . Well, he'd have something to say about that.

"I'm going to have to tell him, you know," Mallory said quietly when she returned to the living room.

Carlson glanced up from the magazine he was reading and looked at her with what he hoped was an open, noncritical expression. It wasn't easy, particularly with Mallory looking all mussed and kissed and generally distracted.

"Telling him about me defeats the purpose."

"He's different," she said succinctly, and threw herself into the chair opposite Carlson. "I can tell you right now he's not after my money."

"Famous last words," Carlson said under his breath. "Your father wouldn't have hired me if he thought all men were as honorable as you think Jake must be."

"Dad might have made the decision to saddle me with a baby-sitter, but I've still got the last say-so over my own life." She leaned forward to tug a brilliant peacock-blue pillow from behind her back and hugged it to her breasts.

"Bodyguard, not baby-sitter, if you don't mind," he said with a smirk.

"Whatever," she muttered. She was feeling cross because she was wondering what would have happened with Jake if her roommate had spent the night elsewhere.

Carlson pushed himself off the sofa and crossed to the wet bar, then poured tall glasses of ice water for the two of them. Returning to Mallory, he put one into her outstretched hand. "Of course you have a say in how things go with your dates," he said mildly. "But it's still my job to make sure they're after your body and not your money."

"What if they want only my mind?" she quipped.

"If they can find it—"

She threw the pillow at his face, missing completely when he ducked. "What's the worst that could happen if I decide to tell him?"

Carlson didn't miss a beat with his answer. "If he's legit, you'll probably scare him off. After all, how many men want to stick around a woman who has more money than they'll ever see in a lifetime? It'll make him self-conscious before you have a chance to get to know each other. On the other hand, if he's not on the up-and-up, he'll look for an end-around. You'll never know if he loves you or your money. Either way, you lose."

"You're such a pessimist." She took one long drink of water, then another. It didn't occur to her to question why Carlson had given her the water, just as she wasn't serious about trying to convince him that it was okay to change the rules for Jake. Three years of sharing the same house had taught Carlson she craved water after drinking anything alcoholic, and she knew Carlson would stick to the ground rules about investigating all her dates as a matter of course.

Before, though, it hadn't bothered her.

"I shouldn't worry about it," Carlson said. "It'll come out all right. When you consider that *we* found *him*, and not the reverse, that's a very good beginning." He wandered over to the bay window, peering out although the light in the living room made it nearly impossible to see anything. "Besides, I kind of feel like I'm playing gooseberry to the two of you."

"You never seemed to mind before," she said, thinking of the times he'd managed to rout any men who'd overstayed their welcome. He was usually fairly sensitive about it, knowing when she'd appreciate the interference . . . and when she wouldn't.

"You were never so . . . involved, I guess," he said slowly. "Seems to me that Jake is more than just another man."

"That's for sure."

"So keeping our relationship a secret from him isn't going to help things along," he said evenly.

Carlson couldn't have been more right, but Mallory had to think beyond her own wants and needs. There was her father, for one. This had all been his idea, to protect her.

"What's to say he isn't another Norman?" She forced the words out, a distasteful reminder of what could happen if she weren't careful.

Her sister Meredith hadn't been careful, and she had paid for it—both financially and emotionally. Now, because of what had happened to Meredith, Mallory lived by a set of rules that was designed to prevent the same thing from happening to her.

"Norman was quite an experience," Carlson agreed. "For your whole family. I thought your dad was going to kill him when he found out."

"Because he married Meredith without divorcing his

first wife, or because he'd already stolen the trust fund Mother had left her?"

Carlson chided her with a single look. "You know your father better than that, Mallory."

"You're right," she said, feeling duly reprimanded for her implied criticism of her father. "He was mad about the money, but Meredith's breakdown really sent him over the edge."

"You didn't exactly come out of the experience scot free," Carlson pointed out. "For two years you wouldn't talk to a man without introducing him to me first."

Mallory grinned because he was right. She remembered the week she'd brought no less than five different names for Carlson to run checks on. He'd told her to pick the one she intended to date that weekend and had thrown the rest in the trash, telling her variety might be safer emotionally but that it was murder on his work schedule. After all, he had other things to do as her father's chief of security besides vet her boyfriends.

That was when they'd become friends. When she'd moved to California shortly thereafter, Carlson had decided it was time for a few changes of his own, and had come along with her. That had been three years earlier, and while he was still receiving a paycheck from her father for keeping an eye on Mallory, he had really stayed because, as he'd once put it, there's nothing like family to give a man a sense of peace.

"He's not another Norman," Carlson said firmly, interrupting her thoughts as he turned from the window. "And if it were my decision, I'd say trust him. My instincts say he's a good man. But—"

"But you'll check him out anyway," she said, smiling at him as he snagged her fingers in his hard hand.

"I'll check him out anyway," he agreed as he took her empty glass and headed toward the kitchen. "In the meantime, I think I'll put in a couple of hours at the computer."

Mallory sighed as she watched him go, then pushed herself out of the chair with a weariness that had snuck up on her blind side. "I can't see how you can stay up all night writing and still look wide awake first thing in the morning," she said to his back.

"If I wasn't writing that book, I'd be up doing something else," he said with a shrug. "More than four hours sleep gives me the willies."

"What happens when you sell it?" she asked when he returned. He had stayed with her longer than he'd first intended, to write the book, he'd said. But when that was done, would he want to go on with other things? she wondered.

"*If* I sell it, you mean," he said, neatly sidestepping her question.

"Would you leave me, Carlson?" she asked, the ache at losing someone she loved already rending her heart.

"I have to get on with my own life sometime," he said gently. "But I won't be leaving you alone, I think. Lately, it seems, you've needed me less than ever before. That being the case, would you really want me to stay?"

He said good night then, leaving Mallory to bank the fire and wonder how she was supposed to answer that.

Five

"It's a great party, boss," Vincent said, pushing his way through the gallery's glass doors to where Jake stood on the sidewalk. "Why don't you go on in?"

"I told you not to call me boss," Jake growled, nervously glancing at the crowd inside the gallery. It was a mob scene, just the kind of thing he hated.

"I could say 'Mr. Gallegher,'" Vincent mused, "but if the kitchen decides to burn down and I need to get your attention, it seems like that would be quite a mouthful."

"So call me Jake," he suggested, ignoring the part about the burning kitchen. The restaurant was the last thing on his mind at the moment. He wished he'd come early with Vincent instead of waiting until it was almost too crowded to get inside.

"Seems a little personal to be calling the boss by his first name," Vincent argued pleasantly, leaning his forearm atop a parking meter at the curb. "And I wouldn't want the staff to call you that. Kind of takes the class out of a place."

"But you call Carlson and Mallory by their first names," Jake said, turning his back on the party to glare at Vincent. The older man was a study in contrasts, impeccably dressed in black tie and dinner jacket, and lounging against the meter as though it were the polished mahogany mantel over a fireplace. Quite a change from the previous night's pink-striped apron.

"Mallory's different and you know it," Vincent said. "But Carlson?" He shook his head, a grin sneaking onto his lips. "Carlson is his *last* name."

"So what's his first name?"

Vincent just grinned wider. "No time to talk now," he said, shoving his hands into his pants pockets as he headed down the street. "Gotta get back to work before that crazy kid gets to the bottom of the list I left him."

"What happens if he finishes before you get back?" Jake asked, raising his voice as Vincent picked up the pace.

"You have to give him a raise," he shouted over his shoulder.

Figures, Jake thought, grimacing as he turned back to the gallery. But then, Vincent had warned him that costs had to go up before they came down, and giving Vincent free rein over the staff had been part of the agreement they'd hammered out that morning.

It had taken Jake only a few hours to realize Vincent counted *him* as part of the staff. Somehow, Jake found himself reduced from decision-maker to "doer"— Vincent decided and Jake did it. Bruised ego aside, Jake was a businessman, and he'd determined right away that if following the orders of someone who knew what to do and how to do it could save his business, then he'd do it.

And maybe he'd have more time for Mallory.

"Are you going to stand out there all night?"

Carlson was at the door, holding it open—either letting in some fresh air or as an invitation for Jake to enter. Jake shook the hand Carlson offered, allowing himself to be ushered into the throng.

"Thought you might have chickened out," Carlson

said, working a path down the center aisle as easily as Jake strolled along an uncrowded beach. Easier, Jake admitted, admiring the other man's natural ability to avoid elbows, wineglasses, and madly expressive gestures as he led the way toward the back of the gallery.

"I had a few things to finish before I left the restaurant," Jake said. Vincent had presented him with a list that morning, and he'd barely had time to accomplish all the tasks before dashing home for a change of clothes. That kid in the kitchen wasn't the only one on a short string.

"Vincent seemed to be in good spirits," Carlson said, waylaying a waiter to snag a glass of champagne for Jake.

"Of course he is," Jake grumbled. "He's having a ball."

Carlson chuckled. "Sounds like he didn't waste any time letting you know who's in charge."

"I should be grateful he didn't fire me," Jake muttered. Saluting Carlson's grinning countenance with the delicate glass, he assuaged his thirst with the champagne, wondering if Mallory would wander by if he stood in one spot.

"I don't get the feeling you're too devastated at being usurped by a new employee," Carlson said, deftly catching a large purple hat that escaped the head of the statuesque blonde next to him. Handling the wild assortment of boas and sequins with respect, he murmured something about the disgraceful lack of elbow room and directed her to a mirror where she might resettle her charming hat.

"I'm more embarrassed than anything," Jake admitted. "But Vincent thinks he can pull the restaurant out of the hole, so I guess I can live with a little humiliation."

"If you can hang on that long," Carlson said. "I understand it takes money to make money."

Jake nodded, but let the remark go by without comment. No sense telling Carlson he could afford to pump working capital into the restaurant from now until doomsday. He wouldn't, though. If, at the end of one year, the restaurant wasn't healthy enough to support itself, he'd give serious consideration to abandoning it in favor of a more lucrative enterprise on that prime piece of real estate.

The possibility of failure didn't seriously occur to him, though. It would be a first, of course, but then he'd never taken on a project quite like this.

"I found him," Carlson said to someone over Jake's shoulder.

Jake didn't have to turn around to know Mallory was standing there. He did anyway, because he'd waited too long to see her again.

Behind him was a woman he'd never met before.

His Mallory was designer jeans and mud and soft sweaters. She was silk and satin, fragile colors, delicate fabrics.

This Mallory was bold, excitingly different, exotic. Following the intriguing diagonals of her dress's wide black and white stripes, his gaze drifted up and down her body, pausing at the curve of her hips where the snugly cut fabric outlined her perfect shape. The dress draped high across her collarbone, leaving her shoulders and arms bare. The full-length sheath defined every curve and hollow, falling to meet a dangerously high pair of heels.

She half turned to smile at a passing couple, and Jake felt as though the world had slammed to an abrupt halt. Her back was bare to the waist, her gown clinging to her by a miracle of tailoring that put more faith in a flimsy golden string than he felt was warranted. He shuddered and was relieved when she turned back to him.

Her hair was glorious. Full and long, it brushed her naked shoulders, tantalizing him with visions of how it would feel when he pushed his fingers through its heavy mass.

This new Mallory stole his breath, aroused his senses, provoked his imagination. But he forgot the package when his eyes caught the movement of her tongue. He stared hard at her mouth, remembering her taste.

It was the first time Mallory had stood still in hours. She licked her lips, suddenly dry as always in Jake's presence, and wrapped both hands around the fragile glass she carried. Moving through the crowd had been easy, exhilarating even as she accepted compliments and tended to business, basking in the gallery's success. The works she'd chosen for the opening were selling faster than she could mark them with red dots, and the demand for more of the same sent her brain scurrying over her list of artists she could show next.

That excitement didn't touch what she felt now, standing before the man she'd been looking for all night.

She'd seen that he didn't know her, then he did. Her eyes caught Carlson's retreating back, and she waited for Jake to say something . . . anything. She couldn't possibly speak herself. Her mouth was too dry. Jake's fault, she realized. He looked good, too good. She wanted to take his hand and lead him out of there. She needed privacy for the things she wanted to do, the way she needed to touch him.

She'd known his hair was black, but not how black as it stood out in stark contrast to his white dinner jacket. His eyes seemed almost translucent, their depths shimmering as his gaze again slid up and down her body.

She could feel the touch of his eyes, and sensed within herself an extraordinary response to his hungry stare. Mallory trembled, knowing that he saw the subtle movement. When he finally met her gaze, she accepted that he could read her mind.

"How long?" he asked, his voice husky with need.

"Until it's over?" she said, knowing she had to stay to the end but wishing she didn't.

He nodded, and she saw his chest heave with a long, deep breath.

"Forever," she murmured, then shrieked as a masculine hand rounded her waist and settled at her hip.

"Love Joseph's watercolors, darling," a man murmured in her ear. "But how ever did you talk him into leaving charcoal?"

Jake eyed the newcomer's hand pointedly, until the hand slipped away. Then he glared at the intruder, letting him know in no uncertain terms that he was never to do that again.

Mallory was more civil. She introduced the men, but wasn't surprised when Andrew spied someone in the crowd and scurried away. "I think you frightened him," she said, and swallowed a healthy measure of champagne to calm her frazzled nerves.

"He's lucky to still have his hand and he knows it."

"I didn't know you were the jealous type," she said, not sure she liked it.

"I didn't either," he muttered. "But one minute we're talking about leaving together and how soon, and the next another man is pawing you. I didn't make the transition very well."

"At least you made it," she said, her light tone belying the hot wave of desire rolling through her body as she thought about leaving the gallery with Jake.

"Don't believe it." Once more he dragged his gaze up the length of her body, thinking about the fragile golden fastening of her dress. When he finally reached her face, he knew she'd forgotten all about Andrew.

Carefully setting his glass on a nearby table, he turned to check the crowd. "I'll wander around by myself. I get the feeling that if I stay beside you, the gallery won't be doing any more business tonight."

"I don't suppose it matters," she murmured, unwilling to let him leave. Of course it mattered, a tiny voice inside her protested, but Mallory wasn't listening.

"It matters," Jake said, and lowered his head as if to whisper something in her ear. Instead, he closed his lips around the delicate outer shell—just for a moment, but long enough for him to feel the tremor that shot through her.

Then he turned and drifted through the crowd.

It was nearly midnight before Mallory pushed the door closed behind the last of the guests. They were all, finally, gone.

Except Jake, of course. And Carlson. Since neither of them could be counted as guests, she kicked off her shoes and padded across the thick carpet to the sofa across from where they'd settled. The men had commandeered the pair of overstuffed chairs and were sprawled in them with ties askew and feet on a low table. Mallory flopped down on the sofa and concentrated on easing off her heavy earrings.

"Too bad we have to open tomorrow," she said, eyeing the wall opposite her and counting the dots, tallying the number of paintings sold. "I'll need at least three weeks to recuperate from those shoes."

"You and the guy you stepped on," Carlson said dryly. "It's a good thing you don't weigh much. You could have put a hole through his foot."

"It wasn't for lack of trying," she retorted, not the least repentant. "My only regret is I did it before he wrote the check. Now I'll have to tell Graham I didn't sell that one because I didn't want it to go to a bad home."

"I think I missed that scene," Jake said. He'd purposely distanced himself from Mallory all night, a noble effort that had apparently left her vulnerable. Then he took another look at the discarded stiletto heels and decided she'd been anything but defenseless.

"You didn't miss anything," Mallory reassured him, The old heel-in-the-foot trick had been one of the first things Carlson had taught her. "But speaking of missing something, shouldn't you have been at the restaurant tonight?"

"I thought Vincent would have an easier time settling in if I weren't there," Jake said. It was as close as he could get to the truth without admitting he was a little overwhelmed by the steamroller he'd hired.

"So he kicked you out," she said succinctly.

"More or less," he admitted, still bemused by his own docility. After ten years of heading a bullish construction company and another five finessing multimillion-dollar investment packages, he was allowing himself to be ordered around by a man he'd actually seen wearing a pink-striped apron!

"I never noticed a Napoleon streak in Vincent," Mallory said. "Perhaps he's just a little excited about being back in the kitchen."

"Kitchen, hell!" Jake snorted. "He's taken over the whole operation."

"Speaking of kitchens," Carlson said, "the caterers left a mess back there."

Mallory sighed, exhaustion sweeping through her body as she left herself relax into the soft cushions. "Remind me to hire different caterers next time," she murmured, then brightened as she remembered relief was in sight on the morrow. "Jeannette said she'd be here to open tomorrow," she said, referring to one of the people who had worked for her in her old gallery.

"We'll still have to do the kitchen," Carlson said firmly.

"Can't it wait until morning?" she pleaded, turning decisions and the like over to Carlson as she snuggled back into the cushions.

She didn't listen for a response as she closed her eyes against the gallery's bright lights. It didn't make sense, she thought. All night she'd waited for the doors to close, for Jake to take her into his arms and soothe the raging fire he'd ignited. She'd been exhilarated by the thought of what was to come, knowing the passion growing between them could be no less powerful than her imagination led her to believe.

No longer could she pretend she didn't know him. True, there were details that he hadn't shared, little things he'd avoided talking about. But she knew the man, or thought she did. And she liked him. The rest of it didn't seem to matter.

Making love with Jake Gallegher was something she very much wanted to do. It wasn't an impulse, but a need that shredded her inhibitions and stole her patience. It would be an experience like nothing she'd ever imagined. The rewards, she knew, would be infinite.

It was unfortunate, then, that she couldn't have moved her left toe if her life depended on it. The mind was willing, she mused, but the body was tired.

"Do you think she's asleep?" Jake murmured, levering his feet off the table.

"Looks like it." Carlson reached for the coffeepot and refilled their cups. "She's worked real hard pulling this place together. And it didn't help that she didn't sleep last night," he added obliquely, eyeing Jake across the cup's rim.

"Too excited about the opening?" Jake asked.

"Or something," Carlson said, his deadpan expression giving nothing away.

Or something, Jake thought. His heartbeat skipped erratically as he remembered the sensual apparitions that had bridled his own sleep to fits and starts, and he wondered if Mallory had been beset by the same images. He didn't speculate any further, though, because he knew the frustration of the night before was about to be repeated.

Jake had known from the moment she'd closed the doors on the last guest that he wouldn't be taking Mallory to his bed that night. He wasn't disappointed, not really. There would be other nights, times when they were both awake.

She'd been high on the excitement of the opening. He wanted her high on him, on them. He wasn't selfish, just careful—he wanted Mallory for longer than just a few nights.

And he wanted her for more than a sensual thrill.

Jake wanted Mallory, the woman . . . the complete woman. Loving, laughing, playing. He wondered if she'd like riding a cable car through a dense San Francisco fog—or if she'd love it, like he did. Did she sleep late on Sunday, or rise with the dawn so she could fully enjoy her day of rest? He wanted to watch her work, as he had that night, and share with her the successes of his own endeavors. He wanted to know everything about her.

Despite the bad reviews, he even wanted to watch her paint.

"Will she wake if I carry her to your car?" he asked, elbows on his knees as he resisted the impulse to join the sleeping woman on the sofa, to pull her into his arms and hold her as she dreamed.

"An earthquake wouldn't wake her," Carlson said. "The car's around back. Give me a minute to lock up."

Jake didn't budge, listening with one ear as Carlson moved through the gallery, snapping off lights and locking doors. After setting the floor locks into the front door, he reached down to snag Mallory's discarded shoes.

Jake finally moved.

She didn't make it easy for him. The moment he pushed his arms under her legs and back, she curled into him, draping her arms around his neck as though he were a teddy bear she could cuddle. Her soft breath warmed him through his open shirt, her breasts nuzzled almost familiarly against his chest. The bare skin of her back singed him and the heat of her body seeped through his clothes, making him wish his hands were free to touch, to caress.

He pulled her closer, taking several deep breaths to control his racing heart.

"She's heavier than she looks," Carlson said, as though misinterpreting Jake's valiant effort to subdue his reactions.

"I think I can manage," he murmured over her head, shifting her in his arms as he followed Carlson toward the back. "Does she do this often?"

"Not enough that I can rely on her for exercise."

Too bad, Jake thought, sliding sideways through the door to the kitchen. Carrying Mallory was something he could get used to. He waited outside while Carlson set the alarm, then followed him to a blue sports coupe parked beside Mallory's Jag.

It went quickly then, lowering Mallory into the passenger seat, fixing her seat belt, and closing the door with the merest of clicks.

"I'll get her to bed," Carlson said as Jake just stood there, wishing he could think of some way he could take her home with him instead of sending her off with another man.

Jake leveled an assessing look at Carlson. "If I thought there was a reason to be jealous, I'd resent what you just said."

"And if I thought she wouldn't shoot me in the morning, I'd let you do the honors," Carlson said, and they shook hands in perfect comprehension.

"Something tells me she'd shoot both of us," Jake said.

Carlson grinned and slipped behind the wheel.

Mallory bent into the brush, scrubbing at the stain at the bottom of the sink.

Hard physical labor hadn't lessened the mortification

she'd felt upon waking that morning, but she'd managed to restore the kitchen to its natural state by the time Jeannette arrived for work, so it hadn't been for nothing.

She'd made promises to Jake, explicit ones, her body language showing him how much she wanted him, her words telling him when.

Not only had she fallen asleep, but he'd carried her to the car and she'd missed it!

Muttering under her breath, Mallory threw the brush under the sink and headed back out front. The mirrors she passed reflected none of the disgust she felt as she wondered if she'd started snoring before or after Jake put her in the car.

Carlson had refused to tell her which, merely stating that she'd been snoring peacefully when he tucked her in.

Mallory pushed her embarrassment aside and spent the rest of the morning and afternoon going over things with Jeannette, running through various artists' catalogues, and double-checking the previous night's sales. None of the paintings from the opening show would be removed for another three weeks, but she needed to make sure there was a ready supply of suitable replacements when the time came. In the meantime, they were deluged by customers who had read about the opening and were eager to discover if any treasures remained on sale.

At least she didn't have to worry about redesigning the exhibit right away, she thought wearily that afternoon, then picked up the ringing phone as Jeannette neatly intercepted another customer.

"Jake called to say he won't be here for dinner after all," Carlson told her.

Mallory held the instrument at arm's length, staring at it for a long moment before bringing it back to rest on her shoulder. Dinner?

"Considering I didn't invite him, I'm not surprised," she said before she was assailed by misgivings. "I didn't, did I?"

"No, I did."

"You what?"

"I invited him for dinner. And he accepted, but I guess things changed, because he just called and canceled."

"Oh." Mallory didn't know which concerned her more—Carlson's invitation or Jake's cancellation. "Any particular reason you wanted his company?"

"Yeah, but don't worry, I'll figure something out." He cut the connection before she had a chance to decipher what he'd meant.

Mallory checked the clock as she watched Jeannette escort the customer to the door, and decided that closing five minutes early wouldn't hurt a thing.

Carlson was up to something, and she intended to get to the bottom of it.

Six

"I called Vincent and he's going to have your dinner ready at eight," Carlson said when Mallory arrived at the houseboat.

"Vincent's cooking here again?"

"Of course not," Carlson said, lifting a vase of roses from the coffee table and moving it to the ledge beside the bay window. "I'm having dinner sent over from that Thai restaurant that just opened. *You're* going over to Jake's."

"Jake's house?"

"Jake's restaurant, Mallory," he said with mock patience. "Why would you be going to Jake's house?" He tucked a tiny arrangement of pink violets into a corner of the bookcase, rearranging the books so the flowers wouldn't be bruised. Standing back, he admired his handiwork. "For that matter, why would Vincent be cooking there when there's so much to do at the restaurant?"

"Can't imagine," she muttered, wondering if she'd be better off going back outside and starting all over. The Twilight Zone was nothing compared to what she was experiencing now. With Carlson talking in riddles and the living room looking more like a florist's shop than a home, she felt uneasily out of place.

"It's a shame Jake couldn't make it tonight," Carlson said, "but I guess some business associate popped up out of nowhere." He eyed an enormous arrangement of poppies and snapdragons that swamped the mantel over the fireplace. Apparently deciding to let well enough alone, he turned his attention to the lilies on the desk. "It sure would have made things easier."

"Would have made what easier?"

"Dinner, of course," he said absently. "She's a little shy, and I thought a group might relax her."

Mallory dropped down into a chair, littering the floor beside it with shoes, purse, and sweater before Carlson could stop her. When he turned from rearranging the lilies, she was comfortably ensconced. Wagging her finger at him, she gave him fair warning. "I'm not moving until you tell me what's going on."

"I told you. You are eating at the restaurant. Peggy is eating here." He pointedly stared at the pile of her belongings. "And you are making a mess."

"You didn't tell me that," she said, politely ignoring his reference to her "mess" as enthusiasm overtook her momentary obstinacy. "Let me stay, Carlson, please," she asked in a tone just short of begging. She was absolutely delighted that the subterfuge in getting Carlson and Peggy together had worked, and she wanted to see the results of her scheming in person.

"No."

"I'll do dishes," she offered eagerly, forgetting her own disappointment that Jake was already booked for the night. It had been a long day, wishing he'd call . . . wondering if he was angry because she'd fallen asleep on him.

"Absolutely not," Carlson said, scooping her things up from the floor and tossing the pile onto her lap. "Move 'em or lose 'em," he warned, acting as though he meant business this time. "I'm trying to make a good impression."

"I don't see why I can't stay," she persisted, trying to get up from the chair without dumping her load back onto the carpet. "After all, you invited Jake, and just because he can't make it doesn't mean I have to vanish." One shoe hit the carpet and she waited for Carlson to pick it up for her, deciding that if he wanted the place clean, he could do his part.

Acting as though she were being particularly dense, Carlson said, "A foursome would have been okay, but I don't think she'll understand you alone."

"You mean our living arrangement is coming under fire for the second time in a week?"

"Not at all," he said smoothly, guiding her toward the stairs with a rather insistent push at the small of her back. "It's just that she's a little shy. However, faced with the prospect of Peggy alone or with you in the room and nothing or no one to distract you, I think she'll be better off alone."

"This isn't your—"

"First date," he said, staying behind her as she climbed the stairs to her room. "And that's as much prying as you've got time for." He gave her a final push that sent her flying into her bedroom. "I want you out of here in twenty minutes."

First date, she echoed silently, keeping the smirk of delight off her face until the door was closed. Gloating was out of the question for the moment. She'd save that part for when she was sure he was hooked.

Carlson hated it when she manipulated him, particularly when it concerned women. Wishing she could extract a few juicy details but knowing better than to try, she pulled off her silk dress and exchanged it for a pair of black wool slacks and a satiny blouse with wide lapels. It occurred to her that she wasn't obligated to go to Jake's restaurant, but when she sat down in front of the mirror to brush her hair, she knew there was no question but that she'd go ahead with Carlson's arrangements.

There was always a chance she'd run into Jake.

The thought sent her pulse speeding. She retouched her light makeup in record time, and still had five minutes to spare before Carlson physically took charge of her departure.

She considered spending the time quizzing him about Peggy, but decided a third degree would probably push him right over the edge.

And thinking of the edge reminded her of Jake.

"It was sweet of Carlson to call you, Vincent." Mallory sipped her ice water, then checked her watch, wondering how she'd spend the next three and a half hours before she was allowed to return home.

"I would have fed you even if he hadn't called," Vincent said, pulling out a chair and making himself comfortable. "After all, this is a restaurant."

"I think he was feeling guilty or something," she murmured, studying Vincent's uniform with a touch of regret. The pristine white chef's jacket and hat looked terrific, but she had a soft spot for how he'd looked in her apron.

"Jake's got some business to take care of," Vincent said. His gaze roved around the room in critical surveillance.

"Can't be helped," she said, but her stomach clenched because she hated not knowing what Jake was thinking. Falling asleep on him was bad enough without having to prolong the agony of not knowing his reaction to her untimely snooze.

Vincent watched as Mallory sampled the creamy soup he'd ordered for her, then dipped his own spoon into the bowl. Muttering something that she interpreted as "stupid assistant" and "too much nutmeg" and "off with his head" between miscellaneous growls of displeasure, he returned to the kitchen.

Without Vincent to keep her company, Mallory studied the other diners. There weren't many, but then, miracles didn't happen overnight. It would take time for Jake and Vincent to turn the place around, months probably.

She wondered if he could afford it.

Mallory frowned, not liking the way that had sounded. She wasn't mercenary, not even a little. With a considerable fortune of her own, she had no need to be. And it wasn't as though she couldn't respect a man without money.

She just couldn't trust him. Not yet, not before Carlson had a chance to do his job.

"I thought Carlson was having a dinner party," a husky voice said, wrenching a gasp of surprise from her.

She colored a little as her heart tried to recover from Jake's sudden appearance, and babbled the first thing that came to her mind. "Four's a party, three's a crowd."

"I know," he said with a note of regret. "And I'd prefer to reduce the number to just the two of us, but I've got a business associate to entertain."

"I understand," she murmured, sighing a little because time and business seemed to be conspiring against them. "Maybe tomorrow?" She looked up at him, certain her heart had stopped because her entire life seemed to revolve around his answer.

He nodded slightly, smiling as he echoed "tomorrow." He was leaning over the padded cushion of her booth, and she knew without a doubt that he wanted her just as fiercely as before. Nothing had changed, she realized, her breathing quickening as his gaze rested on her lips. It was the same feeling she had whenever she was with him . . . only stronger.

She wanted him, intimately, erotically, and to hell with caution.

"Hey, Jake ol' buddy, I thought we were going to eat."

Swiftly masking his frustration, Jake still managed to shoot Mallory a look of pure desire before straightening and redirecting his attention to the man behind him. "I've got a table over by the windows," Jake said, and began to move in that direction.

"And you're going to let this young woman eat all by her lonesome?" Ignoring Jake, the man extended his hand across her table. "Jake thinks we can't talk business around pretty women, but I've always thought it works better that way. My name's Whitaker. Harry Whitaker."

"Mallory Bennett," she said, taking the hand he extended and losing all feeling in her fingers as he vigorously completed the greeting. He was a big man, shorter than Jake but with a pot belly that made him seem larger than he was. Thinning gray hair was combed to the side to conceal a balding pate, and his jovial smile revealed a perfect set of capped teeth.

"I'm sure Mallory doesn't want to sit through a boring business dinner," Jake said.

"I don't want to intrude," she added, smiling at Harry because she liked the fact that he'd finally released her fingers and they weren't broken. "I'm sure you'll get more accomplished without me."

Harry showed his disagreement by sliding into the booth beside her. Pushing the table back a little to accommodate his girth, he looked up at Jake with a grin that dared him not to join them.

Jake shrugged and slipped in on Mallory's other side. "We were almost finished anyway," he said, beckoning to the waiter.

"Good thing too," Harry said emphatically. "The faster this project gets off the ground, the faster we can start making money."

"What kind of project?" Mallory asked, wondering if this was the same thing Jake had been so reluctant to discuss the other night at dinner.

"The one I mentioned before," he confirmed, and shot Harry an exasperated look before continuing. "And as I said then, things aren't at the stage where they should be broadcast."

"Nonsense, Jake!" Harry obviously refused to be intimidated by Jake's warning. "What's Mallory going to do? Shout it from the rooftops?"

"I wouldn't, you know," she said. She was pleased Jake was trying hard to keep from involving her in his business. It would have bothered her otherwise, because then she'd always be waiting for the next step, the moment when he'd ask if she wanted to invest some of her own money on a sure thing.

That was how it had begun with Meredith, but her sister had carried it past that stage. She'd actually married the creep, giving him access to all her money, not just part of it.

"Of course you wouldn't talk about," Jake said, wishing Harry would keep his mouth shut. "But as I told you before, it's mostly a question of timing. I'd rather everything was settled before word leaks out." There was no real reason for Mallory not to know, he told himself, but he'd rather she didn't, not yet.

He wanted her attention on him, the man. Everything else was immaterial.

Harry took the hint with a disgusted snort and backed off long enough to help pick out the dinner wine. He was garrulous by nature, though, and managed to keep conversation lively throughout dinner, telling outlandish stories that centered on his wife—Sophie—and three children. "Ambitious devils," he called them. Picturing a trio of briefcase-toting yuppies, Mallory was astonished to discover the oldest was merely eight. For his most recent escapade, he'd commandeered the home computer in order to put out a weekly neighborhood newspaper.

As Mallory laughed, she noticed she wasn't the only one who had wiped her plate clean. She leaned back with her wineglass in one hand and contemplated the terrific meal she'd had as she listened to Harry's next story.

"Just yesterday," he was saying, "I discovered Sarah—that's my five-year-old—was talking with the computer at work. Can't read yet, but with the voice simulator to help out, she was having a grand ol' time messing around in the files."

"You don't have a password to keep the little gremlins out?" Mallory asked, chuckling some more as she imagined the delight the five-year-old must have experienced.

"Sure," he said sheepishly. "It's written down right there with the phone number. All she had to do was type it in."

"Some security system you've got yourself," Jake said, having a hard time believing a five-year-old could hack her way into a sophisticated system.

"It's all a matter of imitation," Harry said in a stern voice. "They're like monkeys, those kids of mine. Monkey see, monkey do, and all that." Leaning back as the waiter removed their empty plates, he sipped the last of his wine. "Now that we've eaten, I suppose we need to get back to business."

"There's not much left to talk about," Jake said easily. "Nothing we can't do over the phone sometime this week."

Mallory thought Jake was handling the situation nicely, keeping Harry from saying anything indiscreet without embarrassing the man. Still, she was beginning to get a bit curious about the mysterious project.

"I'm surprised you haven't talked Jake into letting you invest in this little scheme of his," Harry said as though he hadn't heard Jake. "I'm sure you could talk him out of a couple of shares if you put your heart into it."

Not for the first time, Jake stifled his irritation at Harry's enthusiasm. The last thing he wanted was to get financially involved with Mallory. It was a complication he didn't need. "There aren't any left, Harry," he said. "And even if there were, I'm sure Mallory wouldn't be interested."

And that, he thought, was that . . . except Harry couldn't leave it alone.

"You can always find more shares, Jake," he said. "Why, I bet if she asked, you'd let her have part of your own. What do you say, Mallory?" Harry grinned at her, oblivious to the underlying currents of uneasiness. "Think you can spare a couple of dollars for a good cause?"

When Mallory didn't immediately reply, he continued. "It's not like you're throwing it away. Why, I'll bet we double our investment in no time at all. Isn't that right, Jake?"

"Only if you liquidate your holdings, and at the appropriate time," Jake said flatly.

"Well, it's not like you couldn't find buyers if that's what you wanted to do," Harry said, bolstering what he apparently considered a marked lack of enthusiasm on Jake's part.

Jake felt it was necessary to emphasize the restrictions, just in case Mallory was getting interested. "It's all in the timing, Harry. Mallory would need to leave her investment intact for at least three years in order to realize the profit you mentioned."

Harry nodded cheerfully. "Three years isn't such a long time, not with a guaranteed pot of gold at the end of it. What do you say, Mallory? Feel like sharing the wealth?"

Mallory sat in complete silence as Harry's persistence finally registered. She needn't have worried that Jake might be setting her up for some kind of investment scam, she suddenly realized. He'd left that to Harry. Jake had lulled her into believing he'd rather not discuss the project, and then, just when her interest was piquing, Harry had stepped in for the kill.

Kill might not have been an appropriate word for whatever con game they were running, but Mallory didn't care. All she knew was she was being set up. How they'd learned about her monied background she couldn't explain, but it didn't matter, not at the moment.

All that mattered was putting a stop to it.

"Kind of hard to say if I'm interested when I don't have a clue where the money's going," she said mildly. Her glance brushed coldly over Jake as she tempered her anger with the desire to get out of there with her pride intact. "And besides, how do you know I would have enough to put into the . . . pot, so to speak?"

Harry smiled. "Class," he said with a broad wink. "You got class, lady. Lots of it. And from where I'm looking, there's only one way to get it. Money. *Old* money." Then, smirking at the astonished expression on her face, he excused himself from the table.

And to think she'd liked Harry, she mused, watching him weave his way across the room toward the foyer. Yes, she'd really liked him.

Not to mention how she'd felt about Jake.

"I'm sorry about that," he said quietly. "He's had a bit over his limit, I suppose. I'll put him in a taxi when he comes back." Jake knew she was upset, but couldn't put his finger on why. It was a cinch it had something to do with talking business, but whether it was because Mallory didn't have enough to invest and was embarrassed, or because she didn't like being pressured, he didn't know. Harry had certainly done enough of that, but Jake knew the older man's enthusiasm for the project simply carried him away.

Mallory pulled her gaze from the empty doorway and forced herself to look at Jake. He was staring at her as though wondering what approach to use, so she made it simple for him.

"Exactly how much does a share in this project run to?"

Jake told her because it seemed the easiest thing to do. Her expression told him nothing about how she took the information.

"And if I decide I'm interested," she said, "will you be able to scrape together a couple of shares for me?"

"If you're interested, I suppose I could let you have part of what I'd held out for myself," he said reluctantly. He hadn't planned on splitting his share, but if Mallory was determined to cut herself in, there was no sense making an issue of it. It was a safe investment, and most likely an extremely lucrative one. As much as he didn't like the idea of getting into a financial relationship with her, he didn't want to seem churlish. "If you like, I'll bring a copy of the prospectus over to the gallery. You can let me know what you think after that."

His words struck a blow she hadn't expected. When it came right down to it, she hadn't thought he'd do it.

But she'd been wrong. Utterly, completely wrong.

"And what if I say I'm not interested?" she asked smoothly, refolding her napkin and pressing it onto the table with fingers that shook. "Will you give it up, or press a little harder, Jake?"

"Who's pressing?" he joked, but his accompanying laughter wedged in his chest as he realized she was deadly serious. Swiftly, he replayed the conversation in his mind and still couldn't figure out what had set her off.

"I mean it, Jake," she said, glaring at him with eyes that were bright from banked tears. "Answer the question."

What the hell was going on here? he wondered. First

she'd seemed interested in the investment, and now she was acting as though she wished she'd never heard of it.

Jake wasn't so sure he ever wanted to hear anything more about it either. He could have sworn he'd been reluctant to offer up part of his own cut of the package, but from the way she was behaving, he'd practically forced those shares down her throat. "If you don't want them, I guess that puts us back where we began," he said, feeling his way cautiously because he knew something was terribly wrong.

Mallory looked at him hard, believing him for an instant because she wanted to, trusting for a moment because she needed to. It was a toss-up, she figured, not knowing enough about him to make a decision, yet wanting to forget the rules and go with her heart.

Because playing it safe had never been an easy first choice for her, she went with her instincts. Smiling unsteadily, she swallowed and reached out to touch his hand. "I guess you're right," she said softly. "We're back where we began."

Jake let out the breath he'd been holding, wishing he knew exactly what had just happened. Clearly, she was uneasy about discussing money. But what did she think was going on that had so upset her?

"How many shares did you let her talk you out of, Jake?" Harry's voice boomed unnaturally loud in the emptying restaurant as he addressed Jake from a couple of tables away. Grinning at Mallory, he strode over to their table and clapped an enthusiastic hand on Jake's back.

Jake tried to diffuse Harry's assumption without reviving his determination to sell Mallory on the deal. "None for the moment," he said. "But if you don't stay out of it, Mallory will think you want to sell her some of your cut. Or perhaps she's going to play both sides and take a little from each of us." He was teasing, at ease now because he knew Mallory wasn't at all interested.

Besides, it served Harry right for trying to sell off part of Jake's personal cut.

He turned to her, grinning, enjoying Harry's momentary discomfort. He did notice that she took her hand from his, and immediately missed its warmth. "What do you say, Mallory?" he asked, still joking. "Ready to plunk down a couple of dollars on our guarantee of a sure thing?"

Harry looked absolutely indignant. "Never!" he exclaimed, then he chuckled. "Suppose I ought to offer to pay for dinner, though. I suspect you're going to end up selling over a few shares to Mallory here when it's all said and done, and you might get the idea it's my fault when the returns start coming in and you have to split yours with her."

Mallory was staring at Jake, the realization hitting her broadside. How close she'd come to believing him! *None for the moment*, he'd said. No, he hadn't given up on the idea. Smiling tightly and avoiding Jake's eyes because she couldn't bear to look into them and wonder if she was right or wrong or just plain stupid because her heart was breaking over a man who was out to swindle her, she excused herself and headed for the ladies' room. Once out of sight, however, she detoured through the foyer and shot out the front door.

It was ten o'clock when she walked into the coffee shop, two hours before she could reasonably return home without breaking her promise to stay away. She ordered coffee, knowing the caffeine would probably keep her awake all night but too listless to request decaf. She drank the first cup steadily, her gaze fixed on the chalkboard with the day's menu scribbled upon it. Idly she wondered if the salmon steak would taste anything like that Vincent had served her that night. It had been superb, as had everything else she'd sampled, including the smidgen of sauteed shrimp she'd stolen from Jake's plate when he wasn't looking.

Her stomach tightened when she thought about Jake, so she set her mind to Carlson and Peggy, wondering if they were having a good time. The Thai dinner certainly couldn't top the one she'd shared with Jake, she mused, then reprimanded herself for not being able to keep Jake out of her thoughts for more than sixty seconds.

Her cup had been refilled before she finally quit avoiding the subject of Jake and what she was going to do about forgetting him. She could move to Alaska, she mused. But then she wasn't sure they had houseboats there, and decided on Seattle instead, because it was enough to change where she lived without having to make other unnecessary adjustments. Seattle, she rather thought, would be houseboat heaven.

Of course, she could always stay in Sausalito and wonder every day if she was going to run into Jake and what she'd say when she did. He wouldn't understand why she'd run out of the restaurant, away from him, but he'd be angry.

Mallory didn't blame him. She'd be angry, too, if the man she was dating accused her of trying to con him out of his money. Not that Jake knew what nefarious deeds her thoughts had indicted him for. It was enough she'd walked out on him without giving him the courtesy of a polite good night or even a slap on the face.

She'd known the minute her car had roared into traffic that she'd made a mistake. It made no difference whether or not Jake intended to swindle her. All she had to do was say no.

What he was, what *she* was, had nothing to do with what was going on in her heart. Inside, where emotions tangled with logic and experience, she knew she needed him. She wanted to be with him, learn about him, share a little of his life so that when it was over she'd have something wonderful to remember.

But she'd thrown it all away when she walked out on him and she didn't know how to get it back.

She was on her third cup when he came.

Concentrating hard on her breathing, which was no longer an unconscious activity, she watched him climb out of his car and stride to the brightly lit entrance of the coffee shop. Only a couple of other tables were occupied, and he didn't spare them a glance as he walked steadily across the room and sat down opposite her.

"It took me a while, but I figured it out," he said, turning over his coffee cup and waiting until the waitress had filled it before looking at Mallory.

"Figured what out?" she whispered, almost afraid to speak because she was certain it wouldn't be the right thing.

"What I'd done to make you walk out," he said evenly. "I guess I was so busy trying to keep Harry from bothering you about the project that I didn't really think about how you might take what I said to him." He waited a minute or so, drinking his coffee in silence until he realized she wasn't going to say anything to make this any easier.

"I don't want your money," he said, gazing directly at her and seeing for himself the relief in her eyes. He was angry for a couple of seconds that she'd imagined what she had, but he was so grateful she was listening that it didn't matter. "I don't want it. I don't need it."

"It doesn't matter—"

"*It matters!*" he ground out. "But I'm making the assumption you have a reason for jumping to that conclusion, and that it doesn't have anything to do with me."

"I thought you were trying to swindle me," she said, almost laughing because it sounded so totally ridiculous, so melodramatic.

"That's the part I figured out," he said, wincing at her words. They wounded him even though he knew they shouldn't. "But by the time I'd put all the pieces together, you'd disappeared. I realized then that you'd run away because you were hurt, and I guess that took me by surprise. You've never done anything predictable before."

"What makes you say that?"

"You mean besides stripping in my restaurant, serving me a gourmet dinner in your home when I arrive to take you out, and falling asleep when you'd promised . . . something else?"

"I did't strip!" she exclaimed, fairly certain that was the only point she could contest with any degree of reliability.

"Moot point," he said easily, waving it off. "But coming back tonight, I'd like to know if you meant it."

"Meant what?"

"The part about going back to where we were," he said softly. "You said it earlier, that we could do it."

"That was before I made an idiot out of myself by running away," she said regretfully. "And I'm not even sure what we'd be going back to . . . or where we were." But, oh, yes, she wanted to!

"In your hallway," he murmured, reminding her of how close they'd been, the heat they'd shared for those moments. "Anything after that kind of fades."

"You don't care about why I—"

He cut her off before she could bring up a subject he wanted buried. "I care, but I don't think it's important right now. I just want to know if—" He stopped for a moment, unable to find the right words. Holding her gaze with his, not willing to risk any confusion, he started again. "I just want to know if you want to be with me."

With the heat of his wanting her turning her blood into a molten river of need, she nodded. Something about Jake made some decisions so incredibly easy.

"I need you to trust that I won't hurt you," he said. "You asked me to trust you about Carlson."

"That's different," she murmured.

"Depends on your point of view. When I'm getting involved with a woman, it's a little disconcerting to have an unknown male quantity breathing down my neck."

She giggled nervously because over the last three years, Carlson's behavior had been much as Jake described. "I see your point."

"All I'm asking you to do is keep your purse-strings closed and trust that I won't try to open them. Is that so hard?"

Yes, she almost said, but refrained because she so very much wanted to please him. "I'll try," she finally said, and she really believed she was doing the right thing.

He hesitated a moment, then nodded. "That's good enough," he said roughly, disappointed that she couldn't give him more, but oddly aware that she hadn't meant to give that much. "For now, that's good enough."

He let out his breath slowly and easily. His relief that she hadn't turned and run again was obvious. There was something, he knew, that stopped her from believing, from trusting, a problem that only time and patience would solve. In the meantime, he wanted so badly to take her into his arms . . . yet he knew he wasn't going to do that at all. When she colored and pulled her gaze from his, he tried to diffuse the charged atmosphere by signaling the waitress for the check.

"How did you find me?" she asked, curious because the coffee shop wasn't located on any logical search grid.

"Carlson figured you'd be here," he said.

"I hope you didn't interrupt anything," she said avoiding his eyes as she checked her watch. She still had another half hour to go.

"I called instead of going over. I remembered he had plans." A sudden dimming of the lights announced the coffee shop was closing. Jake put some bills down on the check and waited for her to stand, then trailed her out to the parking lot without touching her. Even a polite hand at the small of her back was too much to ask of him.

He wanted it all, her soft body trembling beneath his, her cries of excitement echoing in his ears.

Instead, he asked her where she'd left her glasses. Tomorrow, after she'd had a chance to rest and think and rethink, he'd ask her again to take him on trust. At the very least, he planned to discover why it was so hard for her to do.

"In the car," Mallory said, digging in her purse for the keys. Why, she wondered, did she feel as though she were going to get into her car and drive out of his life? He hadn't touched her, not once.

Perhaps, after all was said and done, he didn't want to.

"I've never seen you wear them," Jake murmured. Silently cursing his weakness, he hooked his fingers around the strap of her purse and tossed it onto the car hood. Tomorrow was suddenly too far away. He slipped an arm around her waist, drawing her firmly against his body as he leaned back against the car. "I'll bet they're sexy as hell."

Mallory arched against his arm, her body suddenly hot from the pressure of his legs against hers. But she wanted to see him, needed to know if there was a fire in his eyes that matched the burning inside of her. She tilted back her head to see only shadows.

It was dark around them, and she was blind in that darkness. But sight was suddenly incidental to touch as

Jake stroked her spine, his fingers sensitizing her through the satin blouse.

When his lips found the pulse point at the base of her throat, her fingers dug into the strong muscles of his shoulders. His touch was everywhere, his lips nibbling at her ear, her forehead. She threaded her fingers into his hair, trying to harness his motion as her mouth sought his.

He denied her, pushing his tongue inside her ear as his hands grasped her hips and dragged her closer. She shuddered, knew the cries escaping her lips were pleas for more.

Jake forgot where they were as he relearned the warmth of her body against his. She was soft and firm and so very, very hot, and he couldn't get close enough to the fire. He tasted her skin, caressed its softness, was tantalized by the silk barrier of her clothing. His senses were alive and wanting, almost hurting with the need to see, to touch the intimate wonders of her body.

He wanted to look at her, listen to her as he pushed her to one peak, then another. He wanted to watch her hands as they explored him, feel the warmth as her fingers discovered the hard reality of his need.

The picture was intoxicatingly erotic.

No thread of common sense was left to keep Mallory from wanting him. She knew only need, a deep feeling of incredible passion that drove her to pluck helplessly at the buttons of his shirt.

When the light from a passing car found them, she was struggling with the third button.

Her fingers stilled under the hard grasp of his hand. He held her tightly, tenderly, burying his face in her hair as they surfaced together.

"I can only apologize for the place," he whispered, "but you make me forget . . ."

"I feel like a teenager," she said.

He pulled away, steeling himself for a long night alone

because he'd promised he'd give that to her. "I'll follow you home, honey," he said softly, and helped her into her car when the look on her face almost made him change his mind.

"I don't want to go home alone," she said. She knew she was putting it all on the line, but she didn't care. She wanted to be with him, that was all, and it was so important that he know that.

His slow smile told her how much he'd needed to hear the words. "I've never known exactly where I stood with a woman before," he said with wonder in his voice. "With you, it's all there. You don't hold anything back."

"Except Carlson," she teased, so incredibly happy that she could make a joke out of a sore subject.

"Except Carlson," he agreed solemnly. And because he couldn't do it, he bowed his head to take a final taste from her mouth. After his tongue had dipped into her sweetness and taken when he needed, he spoke against her lips, the movement tantalizingly sensual. "And Carlson had a date tonight, so I think I can afford to let you keep your secret a while longer."

Mallory was home, in bed, before she realized Jake hadn't said when he'd see her again. She grinned then, and set about making several plans that involved way-laying him at one point or another during his day. Grateful that it was Jeannette's Sunday to man the gallery, she stared up at the ceiling and used her caffeine-induced wakefulness to her advantage.

Finding him wasn't the problem, she realized. Convincing Vincent to let him play hooky might be a little tough. She'd give it until noon, she finally decided. After that, Jake was prime kidnapping material and she wasn't going to let Vincent stand in her way.

Seven

"I made a couple of calls yesterday about Jake," Carlson said, although he knew the utter hopelessness of trying to attract Mallory's attention when she was preoccupied with scoping out various piles of junk and treasures. Sunday mornings at the flea market fell into the category of an addiction for Mallory, and while she made a slight pretense at being amiable company, her real efforts were directed to the task of shopping. Still, he thought it was worth a try.

"Say what?" she asked sharply, both eyes trained on Carlson as she strode over to him. "You said something about Jake?"

Carlson grinned. Distracting Mallory from her bargaining rampage had to rate right up there with man's first trip into outer space. "I said I made a couple of calls," he repeated, purposely keeping his voice mild.

"And?"

"And nothing so far." He broke the lock she had on his gaze and stared at a display of wild-looking African masks. "So far, the man is clean."

"I knew that," she said quickly, then flushed because it was like telling a fib. Heaving a sigh, she turned to lead the way down the aisle toward the food vendors.

There she bought Carlson a cafèlatte and herself a cappuccino. They carried the disposable cups with them, and Mallory tried to concentrate on the wares being hawked as she recounted for Carlson the scene at the restaurant. "I guess I feel pretty bad for jumping to conclusions," she ended.

"You shouldn't feel like a jerk," Carlson said, rephrasing her words in such a way, she wondered whose side he was on. "On the other hand, you might have just avoided talking about business altogether."

"I think that's the plan from now on," she said, checking her watch because she didn't want to get behind schedule. It was only nine o'clock, but she hadn't finished her first pass through the flea market yet, and she never left without a quick second go-round. "In the meantime, I'd appreciate it if you'd get some answers before I go out of my mind."

"It'll have to wait until Tuesday," he said. "The guy I need to talk to is on vacation until then."

"So I guess that means you don't have anything else to do?" she asked, arching her eyebrows as she pried into Carlson's personal life.

"It means I don't have time to watch you paw through all the fascinating stuff out here today," he said obliquely, then kissed her on the cheek and sauntered away. Standing in the middle of the aisle with the usual tide of people flowing around her without any urgency, Mallory wished she'd had the nerve to ask outright if Peggy was on the agenda. Deciding that Carlson would tell her only if and when he wanted to, she lowered her gaze to a table of malachite jewelry and paperweights.

After listening to a five-minute sales pitch, during which she learned everything she'd ever wanted to know about the mining of the green stone, Mallory ditched her cup and got down to some serious shopping.

• • •

"Carlson told me you'd be here but I didn't believe it."

Startled and a little miffed because he was always sneaking up on her, Mallory very carefully set the miniature rose tree back on the shelf and turned to Jake. "What is this thing you have about sneak attacks?" she asked. Her gaze drank in his dark good looks as though it had been twelve years and not that many hours since she'd seen him.

"You just weren't paying attention," he said smoothly, taking her arm to move her out of the way of a car driving slowly down the aisle. "I've been following you for ten minutes."

She shrugged defensively. "I guess I get carried away when I'm here."

"Carlson says if you don't get your weekly fix of bargain-hunting, you're impossible to live with." Before she could think of a decent argument to that, he added, "I suppose it's worth remembering."

"I think I've pointed out before that Carlson talks too much," she said, then pulled him in the opposite direction of where he was headed. She always followed the same route through the aisles and just because Jake was there was no reason to buck the system.

It took less than five minutes for her to realize Jake didn't have a flea market personality.

Mallory picked up a calf-length sweater-coat from a pile of clothes strewn on top of a blue tarp and tried it on, experimenting with the sleeves and collar as she looked into a mirror that was for sale across the way.

"You aren't serious about buying that thing?" he asked, looking dubiously at the coat.

"Of course I am," she said. She worked her hands down the side seams and was delighted to discover pockets. She strutted down the aisle and back again to get the feel of the coat swirling around her legs.

"It's too bohemian," Jake said when he realized she wasn't fooling around.

"I can be that," she retorted, smothering a giggle because Carlson would have said exactly the same thing.

Jake lifted an eyebrow but refrained from speaking further. She asked the price, then took the coat off when the vendor told her it was twenty dollars.

"I'd buy it in a flash if he'd take five," she said to Jake, "because it would be a great thing to wear over my mauve miniskirt. But at twenty, it wouldn't get enough use."

The vendor dropped the price to fifteen.

Mallory draped the sweater over her arm and inspected it for flaws. She found a tiny hole up near one shoulder, and managed to get the price lowered to ten when she pointed it out.

"It'll get wet in the rain," Jake said.

"I'll use an umbrella."

"I don't like it," he tried, as though that might influence her.

"But I do," she said with a smile, and asked the vendor if he'd take seven. They settled on eight, and he threw in a hat that matched.

After that she bought a green depression-glass measuring cup.

"Twenty-four dollars is a lot of money for a measuring cup," Jake said dubiously. "You can get a new one for a buck."

"Not like this," she said, delighted with her treasure.

"You don't even cook."

"Then I won't have to worry about breaking it, will I?" she replied smartly, and shoved the newspaper-wrapped cup into her shoulder bag.

The silk scarf was a bargain at ten dollars, she insisted, and it would look terrific with the mauve skirt and sweater-coat. Jake asked her why she didn't try to get the price down to five, and she laughed because everyone knew that particular vendor didn't have to lower his prices. Everything was a steal as it was.

When she bought a large jar of jalapeño-stuffed olives and tried to fit it into her already full shoulder bag, Jake pointed out that she'd apparently reached her max for the day.

She smiled and let him carry the olives.

"Was it love at first sight?" he asked on the way out to the parking lot.

She stumbled and would have fallen had Jake not grabbed her arm. Shaking her head because she knew there was something wrong with her hearing, she asked him to repeat that.

"The flea market," he explained with a teasing smile. "Did you love it that much the first time you shopped one, or was it a gradual addiction?"

Her thudding heard didn't slow with the clarification. She'd almost said yes and she hadn't realized that before! It must have been love at first sight, she mused, staring at him curiously. That explained so much. Perhaps it had taken more than once, maybe a couple of sightings, but there was one thing she was absolutely certain about.

She loved Jake, and all he'd asked her was about the flea market. Laughing, she elected to set aside her startling discovery for a more appropriate time.

"Yes," she finally said, answering two questions at once. "I've always loved the flea market. Don't you?"

"I think I can live without it," he said, putting his arm around her shoulders because she wasn't walking very straight and he thought perhaps her shoulder bag was causing her to list. It was a good excuse to hold her, though, and he kept her at his side all the way to her car.

Mallory shoved her purchases behind the front seat with the rest of the things she'd bought that day, then turned to face Jake. She knew she was grinning like an idiot but didn't really care. "Will you spend the day with me?"

"You don't have to work?" he asked, surprised. Sunday was a big day for galleries.

"It's Jeannette's turn." Her heart soared with hope. "What about you?"

"Vincent said I need some fresh air."

"So you came to the flea market." Leaning back against the car, she studied his face. What would he do, she wondered, if she reached up and touched his lips with her fingers?

"I came to find you," he corrected her, and dipped his head to brush her lips with his. His heart thudded when she cried out as he retreated a couple of inches, so he went back for more, thrusting his tongue deep inside her mouth until her cries were silenced.

Abruptly, he again distanced himself from her, and Mallory couldn't help the reflex that carried her fingers to her swollen mouth. "I like the way you kiss me," she murmured, then blushed beet-red when a couple of passersby laughed. She knew they'd overheard her words.

"We need to go somewhere else," Jake said roughly, and pushed her into her car. "I'll meet you at the houseboat."

After slamming the door with complete disregard for the Jaguar's structural welfare, he strode off in search of his own car. Mallory watched him go, waiting for her breathing to return to normal before putting the key in the ignition.

She was going to tell him about Meredith and Norman and what Carlson had to do with it all, she decided, and why, because of all of that, she'd acted like such a fool last night.

Later, whenever she got up her nerve, she'd tell him, too, about love at first sight and how she'd never believed in it before.

•　　•　　•

Carlson took Jake on a guided tour of the back end of the houseboat, which was devoted to a laundry room and study cum library.

"This is where we keep Mallory's paintings," he said, stepping aside at the doorway to the study so that Jake could get the full impact.

Jake took a deep breath and prepared himself to say something innocuous like "They're not nearly as bad as I expected," or "Interesting if you like that sort of thing." That was before he actually got a good look at them.

They were awful. Absolutely dreadful. His gaze darted from one to the next, and before he could stop himself he gave his real opinion. "She really can't paint, can she?"

"Pretty amazing, aren't they?" Carlson said, leading him to the laundry where the really bad ones were hung over the appliances.

They were like nothing Jake had anticipated. He'd expected some sort of modern art that just didn't appeal to many people. Instead, he found landscapes that looked liked landscapes . . . and also looked as though the "artist" couldn't have had more than an hour or so of instruction or practice.

Jake winced as he saw the childish attempt to paint a sunset with heavy oils. It was as though she had no affinity for the medium, he decided, and wondered where on earth she got the nerve to display them at all.

"Does *she* like them?" he asked.

"Of course not," Carlson said quickly. "She just likes being reminded that while her talent isn't on the creative side of the art world, she's just as successful for what she *is* good at."

"*Very* successful," a female voice said from the hallway.

Both men turned as Mallory came into view, dressed in a summer frock that left her arms and shoulders bare.

"I'd think all you had to do was look at the gallery and know you're good," Jake said, admiring the delightful picture she made with her hair falling around her shoulders and a pair of lilac-rimmed glasses stuck into the dark waves on top.

"Perhaps, then, these paintings are humbling," she said. "And I keep them because every once in a while I get the urge to paint again. And when that happens—"

"When that happens," Carlson interrupted, "she races back here to remind herself it really isn't worth the effort or cost of supplies."

Mallory wrinkled her nose at Carlson and slipped her arm through Jake's, escorting him out of the room before things deteriorated. "Did you have anything in mind for this afternoon?" she asked, and blithely ignored the heated look he shot her. Of course he had something in mind, she realized, but there was something to be said for getting to know each other a little better.

He mumbled a few words she couldn't hear, but instead of asking him to repeat himself, she offered her own suggestion. "I thought it would be a perfect day for the fossil beach."

"Fossil beach?"

"Um-hmm, but you'll have to take an oath of secrecy." She plucked a sun hat from the coat rack, then shouted good-bye to Carlson as she pulled Jake out the front door.

"Why?" he asked absentmindedly. His attention was on the Jaguar Mallory was heading toward, and he was thinking how much he was looking forward to driving it.

"Because if you don't swear never to reveal its whereabouts to anyone, I'll have to blindfold you." She grinned as she opened the driver's door and slid behind the wheel.

"You're not going to let me drive?" he asked with just a hint of groveling in his voice.

"You can't drive blindfolded," she said reasonably, and closed the door.

Jake thought it was a bit eccentric to require oaths and blindfolds, but he didn't care about those nearly as much as he minded not driving. "I'd be careful," he promised, worrying now because he'd suddenly remembered Carlson's warning about her driving.

"You won't get the chance to be careful," she said, then smiled and asked him to buckle up and raise his right hand.

Oaths and most of the swearing finished, Jake asked her why she was so stingy with her car.

"Because it's the first thing I ever bought for myself with my own money," she said, obviously proud of the purchase as she dragged her glasses down onto her nose.

He listened longingly to the contented purr of the engine as she pulled into traffic. "But I've never driven a Jag."

"All the more reason not to start with this one."

"You're selfish."

"And you're pouting," she said, then laughed at his expression when he realized she was right. "Besides," she continued, "I've seen that thing you drive, and I'm convinced you don't treat automobiles with the respect they deserve."

Jake shrugged, unwilling to admit the scarred fender and numerous dents were out of line. "I always figured a car wasn't broken in until it got its first ding. Where's yours?"

Flattening her foot on the accelerator, Mallory decided

she didn't care if Jake spent the entire drive north laughing at the expression of outrage on her face.

She was *not* letting him drive her car!

"So this is where you picked up that collection of petrified sand dollars," Jake said, bending over to check a shell that was half buried in the sand, only to find it was a fragment. Chucking it aside, he wandered closer to the water until he remembered the waves were getting higher. Even with his pants rolled to his knees, he was bound to get wet sooner or later.

"Among other things," she said over her shoulder. "There are lots of petrified rocks and stuff, but you have to know what you're looking for."

"You spend a lot of time out here, don't you?" Looking at her, watching the wind tease the hem of her skirt, her long hair lifting in the breeze, Jake wondered if he'd ever seen anyone so beautiful, so alive.

"Mmmm." She waited for him as he walked toward her. When she felt the weight of his arm across her shoulders, she knew there had never been a more perfect moment in her life. Together, they listened to the waves slapping against their ankles and watched as the sun lowered itself closer to the ocean.

The spectacle of a Pacific sunset was coming, and Mallory knew the best place to wait for it. She urged Jake to hurry, and they sprinted across the sand and jumped into her car. She pulled out of the parking lot and sped along highway one without saying much. Jake talked, though, sharing with her other beaches he'd visited, faraway places where the water was turquoise and the fish the hues of the rainbow.

Even though his words made it all seem real, almost as though she'd been there herself, she wanted to do it all over again—*really* do it—with him.

They had dinner on the balcony of an inn she'd visited

many times, and the small but respected restaurant provided them with a meal that was as memorable as the sunset they'd raced there to watch. Jake talked more, about his maternal grandfather, a Portuguese fisherman; about his father, an Irishman who brought his family to this country and traded on his carpentry skills, until it seemed everyone in the family was somehow involved with a booming construction business.

He told her about his ex-wife, just enough to let her know he'd been married and that it was over long ago. He left out the part about how he'd married her without knowing she wanted only his money and everything it could buy. It didn't matter anymore, he realized in the pause he took to think about it—except the bit about the private investigator his ex had hired after their first date. She'd thrown that little item at him during the bitter predivorce battles, taunting him because she'd known he believed it was love at first sight.

Jake pushed aside the harsh memories. He was with Mallory now, and she had nothing whatsoever to do with the anger he'd felt at that invasion of his privacy. It was over and done with, and while he'd married blindly, the divorce settlement had appropriately reflected his rage at her mercenary tactics.

He smiled at Mallory and explained how his mother had so wanted to see him graduate from college, and how she'd rejoiced when not only Jake, but his two sisters, had met the challenge of various university degrees.

After he finished talking about his family, he waited for her to say something about hers. It was easy for Mallory to tell him about not having a mother, and about a father that drove her mad with his coddling. She mentioned Meredith, and what she was doing now. The rest, the part about Norman, she'd tell him later, she decided. She also skated over the bit about the family money and Carlson's job, because the mood was too easy for that, the pace too seductive.

Perhaps, too, she didn't want to take the chance that he would want to know more. This wasn't a night for cold reality.

Tonight she wanted to know if making love with Jake was as dazzling an experience as she imagined.

When dinner was over, they returned to the ocean, descending the cliff by way of some very steep steps until they were once again walking in the sand, their bare feet making a trail that was easily distinguishable in the light of the moon.

They found a quiet cover hidden beneath the cliff. There Mallory chased the waves, running when they turned on her. Back and forth, she challenged the ocean, sometimes winning, sometimes not.

Jake watched her from his perch on a nearby boulder. He'd been tempted to join her, to share in her laughter as she played in the sand. But it was better this way, watching her, savoring the picture she made in the muted light, coaching from afar.

There were just the two of them on this stretch of sand. On the cliff above, the restaurant overlooked the beach, yet no one else ventured down to sample it. Perhaps the dark kept them away, or something equally insignificant.

With Jake and Mallory there hadn't been a choice. The muted noise of waves crashing against the boulders had drawn them down the path.

She was nervous, Jake saw. In the hush that had followed their intimate dinner, he'd known the moment she realized the barriers were down. No longer was he a stranger to her. Jake knew it, Mallory knew it.

She paused at the water's edge, reaching down to pluck something from the sand. A shallow wave kissed her feet, and she washed the object in the water before straightening. "It's a sand dollar," she said, sprinting to

Jake's rock, holding it out for him to praise. "And it's perfect."

"It's so small," he said. "Smaller than the others in your collection." He wanted a closer look, or so he told himself. He wrapped his fingers around her wrist and lifted her hand closer to his face. It was as perfect as she'd said, and he shared with her the thrill of discovery.

"It's special," she whispered, her eyes shining up at him.

"You're special," he whispered back. He lowered his head and pressed his lips to her fingers. She trembled. The tiny shell seemed in danger of falling, so he slipped it into his pocket before drawing her close.

Mallory felt herself being pulled into his warmth, and she went willingly. He shifted a little, and she slid between his hard thighs, leaning sideways into the body that cushioned her from the jagged rocks. His arms encircled her, hands linking at her hip, a gentle embrace that was totally at odds with the wild thumping of her heart. Her hands rested on one of his arms, her back against the other, and when she dropped her head against his shoulder, she could feel the tension in him.

"Do you think it's right yet?" he murmured into her ear, his lips burrowing beneath a wave of hair to find the delicate skin of her throat.

"I think it's very right," she said softly, then cried out as his tongue drew a wet trail to the hollow behind her ear. He paused to nibble, just for a moment, and Mallory sagged against his arms. It was intoxicating, the things his tongue was doing to her ear. She wanted to surrender to it, lose herself in the pleasure he was giving her.

She fought against the weakness, though, needing to give him strength. She wanted to share, not simply take.

Needing to taste him, to feel the heat of his lips

against hers, she summoned a hidden reserve of will and turned her face until her mouth was under his. He took his time about it, dipping his head to rub his chin across her cheek. Then his lips tracked across the bridge of her nose, skimmed over eyelids that drifted closed.

Her fingers tightened around his arm, clenching the hard muscles as her lips sought his. Again he denied her, and she trembled as he once more returned to the sensitive hollow behind her ear.

Leaving one hand firmly anchored on her hip, he slid the other up her body until he reached her hair. His fingers plunged into the heavy tresses, burrowing until she could feel their warmth against the back of her head.

"I don't think this is a terrific idea," he murmured, his lips brushing lightly over hers before retreating.

"Kissing me?" she asked, eagerly seeking his mouth in an attempt to convince him otherwise.

"Kissing you *here*." He used a gentle force to pull her head out of range. "This is as much privacy as we've ever had together, and I'm not certain I'll stop with kissing."

"Jake, let's stay here tonight, please?"

"Here?" He smiled down at the woman in his arms, avoiding looking too closely at the temptation of her lips. He knew all his good intentions would evaporate the moment he touched his mouth to hers.

"Here," he repeated, "on the beach?" His gaze drifted lazily across the sand and wished they were in Tahiti or Bimini or anywhere warm. The northern California coast, while beautiful, wasn't ideal for camping—not if you didn't come prepared for it.

They'd catch pneumonia, he knew, yet not for a second did he question whether it would be worth it.

"All right," he said. "Here."

Eight

Mallory giggled and pointed toward the cliff. "The inn, Jake," she said. "Up there, where we ate. They have rooms."

"Rooms?"

"Bedrooms," she elaborated, "where people—"

"Don't say it!"

"You're embarrassed!" she shouted, delighted at her discovery. "I'll bet if I could see you better, you'd be blushing!"

"I don't blush!" he said, grateful for the dark. "And I'm not embarrassed at all. I'm just surprised."

"Because I want to make love with you?"

Jake caught her pout with his lips and sent it reeling into oblivion. With nothing left inside him that counseled control, he surrendered to her . . . and to himself.

Mallory seemed to be floating, or drowning. Her stomach must have hit an air pocket, because one moment it was there and the next, it was in her heart.

He'd kissed her before, but not like this, not this wildly, not as though he never had any intention of stopping.

Not that she wanted him to. Lifting a trembling hand,

she circled his neck and tugged his head closer, his mouth harder on hers. She felt him swell against her hip, and sighed when his palm skimmed her aching nipples.

She arched under his caress as he stroked her back once, then again. She was sensitive there, especially down low, in the small of her back. When his fingers discovered that weakness, she shuddered.

She moved against him, caught between his hard thighs on one side, his devilish hand on the other. He finally lifted his head, and she cried out for more.

"Let's go inside," he gasped, holding her steady as he pushed away from the rock.

Mallory nodded, grateful for the arm he kept wrapped around her waist as they walked slowly toward the path.

Jake instantly pushed the door shut behind her because this was a place they could be alone and he couldn't wait another second to begin. Without giving her time to think about what was going to happen, he backed her against the door and covered her mouth with his. She was hesitant at first. He could sense her reluctance in the way she didn't open her lips under his.

When he drew his tongue between them, he felt her first response. Slowly, surely, she surrendered her mouth to him.

Her lips were tender, and his tongue sensitized them further. He drew her bottom lip between his teeth and sucked it into his mouth . . . then let it slide away. His tongue pushed between her teeth to tickle the roof of her mouth, and she suddenly found herself returning the caress.

She tasted him and wanted more.

Her hands reached out for him, grasping his shoulders with the intention of pulling him close. But he withstood her efforts until she whimpered at the coldness she felt without him.

"If you're sure," he murmured against her lips, "but I want to hear you say it."

He stood back from her, withdrawing several feet until she could see only his shadow in the darkened room. The moon was still bright, but the curtains were drawn against it, leaving vague shapes that were barely discernible to her poor night vision.

"Say what?" she asked dazedly. He wanted her to talk?

"That this is what you want," he said, retreating another foot when she pushed away from the door. "That it's me you want." He backed up a little more and found himself near the curtains. Reaching up, he dragged them open, exposing a bay window above a padded bench seat. He leaned across the seat and pushed open the window.

"I want you," she said softly.

He didn't speak as he shrugged out of his jacket. When it hit the floor, the shoes she'd thrust into the pockets thunked loudly in the silence, but he ignored it. Instead, he held his hand out to her and waited for her to come to him.

She took the first step eagerly, then another. A four-poster was on her right, she noticed, and there was an old-fashioned vanity with a ruffled skirt on her left. Another step, toward the sea beyond the window, and she was closer. Moonlight streamed in through the open window, illuminating the man who was waiting for her just a few feet away.

Then, suddenly, there was nothing between them. Mallory took the hand he offered and felt herself drawn into a circle of warmth that was so familiar, yet so excitingly new. She moved against him, pressing her open mouth to his shirt. His heart thudded against her lips.

Her fingers worked at the buttons, slowly because his hands were roaming across her back, distracting her as they plunged down to that hollow that excited her so, rising again under the fall of her hair to a place she'd never known was so sensitive. He soothed, she worked the buttons. He dragged his fingers lightly across the nape of her neck, and she grasped his shirt to keep from falling.

At last she pulled his shirt from his trousers and pushed it away from his shoulders. Jake shrugged out of it and resumed his stroking. She felt his hands harden their teasing caress, and arched against him when his fingers grasped her dress and pulled it and her slip up to her waist.

"The window," she breathed, then moaned at the heat of his palms against the bare skin of her lower back.

"There's no one out there but the fish," he said, pushing his hands inside her silk panties.

He cupped her bottom firmly, digging his fingers into her soft flesh and pulling her against him, needing to soothe the heat that was building inside him. He held her there, just for a moment, and knew the attempt to slow it down had failed.

He wanted Mallory, and he wanted her then.

Cursing his impatience, Jake silently promised her the next time would be slower as he pushed her panties down her legs. Then his fingers grasped the fabric at her waist and lifted it over her head.

She was naked in the moonlight, shivering at the suddenness of his actions. Her breasts weren't large, her waist wasn't tiny, her legs weren't any longer than necessary . . . but everything, added together, made a picture that left him breathless.

He swallowed hard, almost afraid to touch, knowing there was nothing that could stop him. He folded her back into his arms and stroked her shivering body, intending to give her what comfort he could before he lost his mind altogether.

But Mallory didn't want comfort.

Her mouth opened against him again, this time on the bare skin of his chest, which was covered with soft, dark hair. Her tongue drew hot, wet swirls around his nipples, and she tasted the thin film of sweat on his skin as she dragged her tongue across the bunched muscles of his shoulders.

When he thrust his hands into her hair to hold her for his kiss, her fingers traveled downward, through the springy hair of his chest, down to the waistline of his trousers. Her tongue argued with his, fought a battle that was wet and exciting and very, very erotic. He thrust inside of her, setting a rhythm that drove her mad, then retreated to suck her tongue into his mouth.

When her lips were swollen and almost too sensitive to touch, he left her mouth to excite her in yet another way. He was fast and smooth, taking a nipple between his teeth, biting just enough to provoke her deep cry of excitement, then opening his mouth to cover her breast. The suction drove her frantic, and her fingers fumbled at the buttons of his trousers.

He didn't stop what he was doing to help her, because he wanted to know he could drive her mindless, send her to heights of ecstasy without entering the hot core of her. At the rate those little cries were flowing from her mouth, it was working.

Impatient, wanting to know more, he let his fingers wander down her back, lightly caressing the sensitive hollow, then suddenly slipping his hand across her hip and around for another, more intimate caress. His arm circled her back to support her as his fingers threaded through the tight curls he found there.

He didn't take his time, but pushed ahead, needing to know if she was as eager as he. There was no question of that, he realized. A single touch told him she was hot and wet and ready. Another stroke produced a quiver that weakened her knees, and he did it again, fully supporting her as he marveled at her total responsiveness to his touch.

She'd managed to undo the buttons of his trousers, and the zipper finally quit resisting, but Mallory couldn't bring herself to pull away from his hungry mouth, so his trousers remained in place. When she felt his arm behind her knees, she was relieved he understood her inability to stand any longer.

He didn't carry her far, but laid her down on the window seat, in the moonlight, beneath the open window. She shivered, not because of the breeze but because of him, her body still vibrating from his caress as she watched him kick off his shoes and push the trousers down his hips.

He was magnificent, everything she'd imagined . . . and more. Not that he gave her much of a chance to look, because he'd no sooner rid himself of his clothes than he returned to her.

There wasn't much room, but it didn't seem to matter. Jake carefully lay down against her, allowing bare skin to meet bare skin fully, for the first time. Mallory suddenly found herself being rolled and lifted, until he was staring up at her and she was lying across his chest, her legs tangled with his, her hair sweeping across his shoulders and face.

"You're sure this is a good idea?" she joked, breathless at the feeling of control she had in this position.

"I know it is," he murmured. He wrapped a strand of hair in his fist until she was forced to lower her head to meet his. "And this way we won't fall off."

"How do you figure that?"

"Physics, my dear," he said, rubbing his lips across hers. "Something to do with the center of mass," he explained in a sexy, scholarly voice. "And besides, I thought you'd like it."

"I think I will," she whispered, and nibbled at his ear as she felt him stirring against her.

"Will?" he gasped.

She opened her legs over him. "Will," she said firmly, raising herself to her knees. Using her hands at his shoulders for balance, she gently, carefully, lowered herself onto him.

Her cry was long and low and lush. Mallory shut her eyes against the rapturous sensation of his body slowly entering hers. Steadied by his hands at her hips, she took him into her, to a place neither had ever imagined existed.

"I do," she breathed, though it took enormous effort to pronounce each word.

"You do what?"

"I like it . . . like you said I would." Taking a deep breath, she forced her eyes to open. The burning passion in his gaze made her burn too. And because she was so very happy, it made her smile. "And I think you like it."

"No kidding." He groaned as she contracted some very critical muscles around him. After taking several deep breaths, he fixed her with a daring look. "I might let you do this again sometime."

"You might, huh?" she said, lifting herself so that he was no longer buried deep inside her. His hands clenched at her hips, and she saw his eyes narrow as he pulled her back down.

It was Mallory's turn to sweat.

She might have been on top, but position had nothing to do with control. Jake lost his, too, the ache inside him demanding release. Tangling his fingers in her hair, he pulled her head down to his mouth and pushed his tongue between her lips. They took a moment to enjoy a simple kiss, one tongue gliding across the other, lips and teeth nibbling at will.

But when Mallory pulled his tongue between her teeth and began a gentle suction, Jake could play no more.

His hands lifted and pulled her hips into a rhythm he could no longer resist. Her mouth left his and she straightened, riding him, losing herself in the pulsing beat, gasping when his one hand left her hip to stroke her to a greater excitement.

She cried out when it became too much, when she lost control of the rhythm and felt herself shooting through the stars. The world exploded around her, and she would have fallen if not for the hands that gripped her wrists.

She felt herself melting downward, falling, until his chest cradled her. His heaving chest, she noticed, thinking she should move aside to let him breathe. She had no strength to do so, however.

With her face against his chest, she could tell when his heart slowed. Her own was still thumping erratically when he spoke. "I think we're damn lucky we didn't fall off this thing," he said, and for the first time she noticed he'd dropped one foot to the floor for balance.

She giggled, turning her head to see his other foot anchored on the windowsill. "I think it's safe to say we got a little carried away."

"I guess you're right." He blew out a sigh of relief that they hadn't ended up on the floor, although he wasn't sure he would have noticed. "I've never lost it like that before," he said, shaking his head. "Intense, almost—"

"If you say metaphysical, I'll gag!"

"I was thinking more along the lines of ethereal."

"I'm not sure that's not worse," she teased, and licked a bead of sweat from his shoulder.

He lightly swatted her bottom. "You're making fun of me."

"Just because it's so easy." She snuggled a little higher so her mouth was level with his. Brushing her lips across his chin, she felt the breeze on her back and knew it was raising goose bumps. "I don't suppose you'd be interested in moving to the bed?"

"Only if you move first. I don't have the strength to carry you." He wasn't sure he could walk, but he didn't say that. No sense giving Mallory something more to kid him about. Taking a fortifying breath, he rolled her toward the wall and slipped out from under her. When he was on his feet, he grabbed her hand and started walking.

"At least wait until I'm on my feet!" she protested as he nearly pulled her off the cushions butt-first.

"Sorry. Forgot."

"It's okay." She found her feet and placed them firmly on the floor. Surprised that her limbs were following her commands, she took advantage of the trend and stood. "I guess you're pretty tired."

Jake turned from his contemplation of the bed. Slowly, so that she couldn't miss it, he let his gaze drift down her body, pausing for a moment at her breasts, her belly, the curls between her legs. By the time his eyes returned to her face, she knew she'd made a mistake.

Jake was never *too* tired. She gulped, then pasted on an innocent expression in hopes he'd not take her words as a challenge.

He didn't buy it. "If I didn't know better, I'd say you wanted more," he murmured, tugging her hand now, pulling her behind him as he crawled between the sheets.

"Sleep!" she said quickly. "That's exactly what I need."

"Then I suggest you keep that mouth of yours in check." He hauled her into his arms, then waited until she was comfortably snuggled against him before pulling the comforter around their shoulders.

"Jake?" she said sleepily against his chest.

"Hmmm?"

"There's something I was going to tell you," she

mumbled, and turned onto her other side so that her back was warm against his chest. It was perfect, the way they fit together, she mused. Forgetting she was in the middle of telling him something very important, she let the peace of his embrace lull her into sleep.

"Mallory?" Jake asked softly, but he knew she wasn't with him anymore. She was snoring softly into the pillow, and he was relieved because he couldn't imagine anything better than falling asleep with her in his arms.

Talking would have been redundant at this point, he thought, because they'd already showed each other what they felt. Words couldn't have made that glorious feeling any plainer.

Love, he discovered, was so much more than a four-letter word.

Jake tossed her dress and panties into the bathroom and pretty much threw Mallory in after them. "And hurry!" he urged. As he pulled the door shut, he hoped she wouldn't curl up on the floor, because then he'd have to wake her up all over again.

"I really hate this," she muttered loudly enough for him to hear, but with care not to awake the rest of the inn's patrons.

"I know, honey," he said, pulling up his trousers and tucking in his shirt. "But I promised Vincent I'd be there when the vegetables were delivered this morning and would help the new morning cook open up."

"What do you know about opening up a restaurant?" she grumbled.

"I have a key."

Having dressed in record time because she didn't intend to stay awake any longer than it took to drive back to Sausalito, Mallory exited the bathroom and took the shoes Jake held out to her. "I can't imagine why you have to do all this at four-thirty in the morning," she said. "It's not even light out yet."

"Then we won't have to worry about who'll see you with your hair sticking out," he said, then chuckled as he sidestepped the punch she aimed at his shoulder.

"You could lend me your comb." As she raked her fingers through her disordered mane, she took care not to look too hard at Jake. She thought he looked rather dashing for a morning after, and she didn't feel like making the comparison.

"No time," he said, draping his jacket around her shoulders as he led her out of the room. "And besides, I think you look beautiful," he added, and dropped a kiss on her cheek.

"You're just saying that because you know you're supposed to," she muttered as she unlocked her car. The leather seat was cold under her legs and she immediately punched the heat button after turning on the engine.

"If I told you that pulling you out of bed without making love to you again was the hardest thing I've done this decade, would you believe that?" he asked softly.

"Depends."

"On what?"

"On when you intend to make it up to me." She leaned across the console and planted a loud, wet kiss on his lips.

Grinning at her wickedly dancing eyebrows, Jake pulled her head back into range and gave her a kiss that was considerably more involved, letting her go only when he realized they were still in the parking lot and his resolve to leave was weakening.

"Now get this junker in gear," he commanded, handing Mallory her glasses from the dash. "Vincent will ground me if I'm late."

Taking the threat as fact, Mallory raced the Jaguar

along the nearly barren highway, rubbing the sleep out of her eyes as she looked forward in anticipation to the night ahead.

"I'm glad you stopped by," Carlson said.

"That's only because you needed help moving this table," Jake said. He grunted as he lifted it over his head and followed Carlson up the gallery stairs to the second level.

Carlson tried not to laugh, but he couldn't completely smother his grin. "There's that," he admitted, checking over his shoulder as the table drew even with the mirrored wall. In moments they had the table in the middle of the room, and the two men stepped back.

"Mallory looks like she didn't get any sleep last night," Carlson said.

His comment surprised Jake, because he hadn't thought Carlson would say anything at all. And since he still hadn't figured out the relationship between the two of them, he wasn't sure if it was a criticism or a warning or just a simple observation. He looked at the other man and saw that he was grinning with approval.

"She slept," he said firmly. "I just had to roust her out a little early."

"I've lived with her for three years, and the only thing she gets out of bed for before eight is the flea market," Carlson said dryly.

"I'll keep that in mind," Jake said, his smile widening. It was clear that while Carlson and Mallory were close in a way he didn't understand, it wasn't going to affect Jake's relationship with her.

"I suppose she'll want us to bring that silly-looking thing up next," Carlson said abruptly, referring to the sculpture that was to occupy the table.

Jake had seen the sculpture, and shook his head, baffled. "I thought she had better taste than that." He wandered over to an odd-looking thing hanging on the far wall. It was framed, and technically he supposed one would call it a collage. He wasn't sure, though, because he'd never seen anything quite like it. It was composed of pieces of wood and metal and scraps of torn and stained fabric that were glued or nailed to a graveled surface. "I guess this matches the piece of junk she's putting on the table."

Carlson walked over to stand beside him and told him what the thing on the wall cost. Jake was making gagging noises as he continued. "I don't think this is so much a matter of taste," he explained, "as what she thinks will sell. And this piece of junk," he said, touching one of the wooden projectiles that protruded several inches from the frame, "will sell."

It came apart in his hand. Not all of it, just an inch or so from the piece he'd touched. Sharing with Jake a look of horrified disbelief, he tried to fit it back on. "Glue," he said urgently. "Get some glue before she finds out!"

"How can she *not* find out?" Jake said, trying not to laugh but failing miserably when he saw the panicked look on Carlson's face. "You just wrecked a valuable piece of art!"

"Art!" Carlson sputtered. "You called this a piece of junk!"

"That was before you told me what it cost."

"Just quit arguing and get the glue before she comes up here!" Carlson bent back to the picture, working the two pieces together and waiting for them to magically bond.

"What do you need glue for?"

They moved in unison to obscure Mallory's view of the damaged collage as Carlson tucked the splintered end out of sight behind his back.

"The table leg," Carlson ad-libbed.

"What's wrong with the table leg?" she asked, frowning suspiciously at the united front Jake and Carlson were presenting.

"It needs some glue," Jake said, smiling ingenuously. "Why don't we leave Carlson to take care of it? I have only a little time for lunch." He tried to hustle Mallory out of the room but she wasn't having any of it.

"I know that expression on your face, Irwin James Carlson," she said, ignoring Jake's guffaw at learning Carlson's first names. "You're hiding something behind your back. Give it to me."

"Irwin James?" Jake said, laughing aloud and feeling perfectly safe in doing so because Carlson was busy enough with Mallory for the moment.

"Give it up," she demanded. Hands on hips, she advanced to within a hair's breadth of her guilty-looking roommate.

Carlson heaved a deep sigh and opened his palm to reveal the jagged bit of wood.

"What's that?" she asked.

"The table leg?" he tried without much hope in his voice.

Mallory was much sharper than that. She firmly pushed him aside and locked her gaze on the collage. "You broke it!"

"It fell off!"

"Same thing! Do you realize what you've done?"

"It was an accident," Jake said quickly, for it seemed Carlson wasn't going to get off with just a slap on the wrist. He needed to redeem himself, too, for laughing about the Irwin James thing. "And besides, he didn't do it. I did."

"*You* did it!" Switching to the new target, Mallory fixed her accusatory stare on Jake and prepared to tear a few strips off his hide.

Behind her back, Carlson opened his mouth to argue, but stifled the urge when Jake shot him a quelling look.

Shrugging, he leaned against the table to watch the fireworks.

"Nothing to get excited about, Mallory." Jake closed the distance between them and rested his hands on her shoulders, flexing his fingers over the tense muscles he found there.

"Nothing to get excited about! That thing cost big bucks, and I'm responsible for it!" She glared at him for a long moment, trying to stay detached from the gentle persistence of his hands, yet failing bit by bit as his impromptu massage stole the balance of her tirade.

"I'll buy it."

She gasped, not sure she'd heard him correctly. "You'll buy it? But it costs—"

"I know," he cut in. "Big bucks. We'll hit the details later." Trying not to think about where he'd hang the thing, Jake kept a smile pasted on his face. The money wasn't important, but buying junk went against the grain.

Then again, now he had something to donate to that charity auction next month. With that one positive thought in mind, his smile became genuine.

"I like it," he fibbed when she didn't say anything. "I *want* to buy it." He swallowed, then felt a bit better as he remembered the collage would have to stay in the gallery for a couple of weeks until the show was over. After that he could turn it over to the auction committee.

"I don't believe you," she said stubbornly. "Can you afford it?" she asked in the next breath.

"Now, *that's* a tacky question," Carlson muttered from across the room.

Mallory ignored him and looked hard at Jake. If it was going to put him into the poorhouse, she wouldn't consider letting him have it.

"Trust me" was all he said, although his bland expression could have hidden anything from consternation to amusement.

She almost smiled, but hid it behind a suspicious glare. "Now, where have I heard *that* before?"

He didn't answer. Instead, he quirked an eyebrow as though waiting for her next question.

Mallory mulled it over for a moment, not believing for a second that he liked the collage. "Joseph is never going to forgive me for letting it be destroyed," she said bleakly, referring to the temperamental artist.

"Once it's sold, I don't think you have to tell him anything," Jake said firmly. "And besides, it's not destroyed. Give Carlson a chance to glue it back together and it'll be like new."

Carlson roused himself to help close the deal. "Let's get real about this, Mallory. No one, absolutely no one, is going to be able to tell the difference."

"*I* can tell the difference," she protested, not sure why she felt she was being railroaded.

"That's why you're the gallery owner and we're the peasants," Jake said patiently. "I bet you wouldn't be so mad if you'd done it."

"Of course I would," she lied. "But then, I wouldn't have broken it in the first place." She ducked out from under Jake's soothing caress because he was driving her mad with those little circles he was making on her shoulders, and walked back to the collage, staring closely at it. Perhaps with a little glue . . .

Jake was ready for some fresh air. "I think I'll go on to lunch. Join me, anyone?"

"Sounds good to me," Carlson said. "Mallory?"

"Can't," she said. "I just let Jeannette go out for a sandwich."

Carlson shrugged and slipped out of the room, saying he'd meet Jake out front.

"Too bad," Jake said, managing with two words to let her know he was sincerely disappointed. "I guess I'll just have to wait until dinner."

Mallory nodded a little forlornly. Dinner seemed such

a long time away, but there was nothing to do but soldier on. She whipped up a smile for him. "I'll meet you at the restaurant after I finish here."

"Good enough," he said gruffly. He stepped through the door to the stairs, then turned. For just a moment he let the desire he was feeling show in his eyes.

In the next instant he was gone.

Mallory took deep, even breaths, but knew it was fruitless. Nothing could possibly calm her racing heart—nothing, no one, except Jake.

And that, she knew, would happen only in the calm after the storm.

Nine

"I forgot the hammer," Mallory said. She briefly considered substituting her shoe, then remembered she'd worn sandals with narrow high heels. Turning to Vincent, she asked if he wouldn't mind finding her one.

"I still think you should ask Jake before you hang that . . . thing in here," Vincent said, eyeing the collage she'd propped against the wall of the restaurant's foyer.

"Nonsense," she retorted. "Then it wouldn't be a surprise."

"No kidding." Still, he headed down the hall to the office, returning a couple minutes later with the hammer.

Mallory smiled her thanks, then frowned when she practically had to pry Vincent's fingers from the wooden handle. He was stalling, she understood. But he was no match for the streak of stubbornness that had long been one of her more enduring traits, and soon she was pounding the picture hanger into the wall.

"Help me lift it," she said, "but be careful. It's fragile."

"I don't think this is in my contract," Vincent mumbled. He bent down to help anyway, figuring correctly that Mallory was going to get it hung one way or another.

She was standing across the room, eyeing the collage and directing Vincent which side to raise or lower, when Jake strode into the foyer.

"What's that thing doing here?"

"Not my fault, boss. She made me do it." Vincent picked up the hammer and started toward the kitchen. Passing Jake, he added, "You know what she's like when she gets an idea in her head. There's no stopping her." Without waiting for a reply, he left.

His absence went unnoticed.

"I thought it had to hang in the gallery for the duration of the show," Jake said, trying to hide his dismay. The last thing he wanted was to let her know he hated it. Then she'd insist on taking it back and Carlson would be in the doghouse again, and Jake really didn't think he deserved that. Besides, Carlson would probably bring up the subject of how Jake had subjected his Christian name to ridicule, and there was no need to get into a huff over something Jake sincerely regretted.

Carlson wasn't to blame if his mother had been misguided enough to hang a tag like Irwin on her son. Nor was Jake at fault for laughing at it, but that was beside the point.

"It'll get just as much exposure here," Mallory said, hoping Jake wouldn't pry into her reasoning too deeply. She'd only wanted to get it out of the gallery before Joseph saw the damage. A temperamental artist in a rage was something to be avoided at all costs, and she didn't want Jake to feel too bad about having to purchase a ruined masterpiece. "Besides, I think it looks pretty terrific on that wall," she lied, and kept her back to Jake as she moved to straighten the frame. It looked awful and she knew it, but perhaps she could convince him to hang it in the laundry room after an appropriate time.

Just because other people liked Joseph's work didn't mean she had to!

"Is this your way of getting back at me because I made fun of your paintings?" Jake asked, a gleam of speculation in his eye.

"I thought you liked it!"

"I don't."

"But Jeannette said you wrote her a check—"

"A *big* check," he clarified, just so she knew he could tell the difference between a few dollars and a major investment.

"Then I guess I'll take it," she said, grinning.

"Take what?"

"The credit, of course."

"For what?"

"For getting back at you for making fun of my paintings," she said patiently, and they shared a smile because it felt so good being together.

"Mallory! Fancy finding you here!"

As she turned in surprise at Carlson's voice, Mallory's hand connected with something sharp. There was a loud snap, followed by her cry of dismay. Reaching down, she picked up a two-inch splinter from the carpet.

"Oh, no!" she wailed, holding the fragment gingerly in her palm.

"Oh, yes," chorused a pair of masculine voices.

"Oh, no!" she cried again.

Jake could no more stop the laugh that erupted than he could stop breathing. Carlson didn't have any better luck, although the woman beside him managed only a mystified half grin.

"Hi, Peggy," Mallory said nicely before leveling a menacing look at the two men, as though she were considering nailing them to the wall beside the collage. She waited until Peggy returned the greeting, though, before turning back to the emergency at hand.

"Where's the glue, Jake?" she demanded.

Unfortunately, that only provoked more laughter. Shooting another malevolent look at the two of them, Mallory stomped down the hall toward the kitchen.

"I'm going to burn that collage someday," she muttered. Smiling grimly at the warm feeling of purpose that gave her, she shoved open the kitchen door.

"Where'd Carlson go?" Mallory asked.

"He left." Taking the tube of glue from her hand, Jake proceeded to reaffirm the integrity of the collage.

"He left without giving me a chance to talk to Peggy?" Peering over his shoulder as he dabbed glue on the broken piece, Mallory had second thoughts about the wisdom of hanging such a valuable work of art in such a high-traffic area.

"Carlson probably didn't want you to grill Peggy." Straightening, Jake recapped the glue and tossed it onto the reception podium.

"As if I would." She followed Jake back down the hall, thinking that a rope and stanchion set in front of the collage would do wonders for her peace of mind.

"Carlson appears quite smitten, if you ask me." Reaching a door marked "storage," Jake pushed it open and entered. Milliseconds later his hand reached out and yanked Mallory inside before slamming the door shut.

It was cool and dark inside, the heavy odor of industrial-strength cleaners permeating the air. Mallory snuggled securely in Jake's embrace and giggled.

"What's so funny?" he asked, dipping his head for a kiss but ending up with a mouthful of hair. Trying to pretend that's what he'd intended, he pulled a few strands from his tongue and tried again.

He got her nose on that try.

"Hardly the most romantic setting," she chided him,

then lifted her head to find his mouth. She succeeded where he'd failed, and she couldn't resist teasing. Touching his lips with her own, she arched back to keep the caress light.

"So you don't want to kiss me in the closet?" he murmured.

"Seems as though we could at least try for your office." Leaning forward, she touched her tongue to the corner of his mouth before tracking across the light stubble on his chin.

Chasing her lips with his own, he sighed. "I don't have an office. Vincent took it over."

She laughed at the chagrin in his voice, then turned her head just enough to find his mouth, provoking a sensual groan from him when her teeth fastened onto his bottom lip. She lost herself in the thrill of the exciting caress, pulling him to her, shuddering as his palms began a hard massage at the base of her spine.

They nearly managed to forget where they were. Recall came with the arrival of a busboy.

They jumped apart as the door swung open, blinking owlishly at the light that streamed in from the hallway.

"Excuse me." Acting as though he were used to finding the storage room cluttered with kissing couples, a white-jacketed young man flipped on the light and headed straight for the corner where the clean linens were stacked. After filling his arms with an assortment of napkins and tablecloths, he crossed back to the door and asked if they wanted the light off or on.

"Leave it on," Jake growled.

Undaunted by Jake's stare, the busboy smiled politely and left.

"No need to bark at him," Mallory said. "How was he to know you don't have anywhere to conduct business?"

"You're not business, you're personal." Snagging her wrist, Jake pulled her back out into the hallway, not releasing his grip as he made his way toward the kitchen.

"Personal as in private?" she asked, throwing out an arm for balance as he dragged her through the kitchen. Dodging busy waiters and cooks, they threaded their way through the narrow aisle. Rushing past Vincent, Mallory managed a breathless "bye!" before Jake pulled her out the back door. He kept moving until they reached her car.

Swinging around, he cupped her face in his hands, his thumbs tilting her chin up until her mouth was beneath his. He kissed her deeply, startling her with the sudden heat that gathered deep in her belly. He stroked her mouth, showing her without words the passion she fired in him.

Finally, when the tremors he provoked made it nearly impossible for her to stand, he lifted his head. "Personal as in intimate," he murmured, and leaned down for another fast kiss before setting her away from him. "No more parking lots, hotel rooms, or closets. I'm taking you home."

"The houseboat?"

"My home. My bed. Got a problem with that?"

"No. I drive?" she asked, pulling the keys out of her pocket.

"If you must." Buckling himself into the seat beside her, he gave directions, then settled back to contemplate the evening ahead.

"You didn't tell me you lived on the water." Mallory stepped through the french door and onto a flagstone patio that extended the full length of the house.

"*You* live on the water," Jake said, following her as she crossed to the low wall that surrounded the patio. "I merely live next to it."

She shrugged. "Same thing. It's still in your back-yard."

"Cuts down on mowing."

Sitting on the wall, she looked up to investigate the exterior of the house. The two-storied dwelling looked new, she decided, and substantially expensive. The interior was much the same, its furnishings implying a quiet opulence that she hadn't overlooked on her way through to the terrace.

"I like it," she said simply, wondering how she'd had the gall to imagine Jake was out to steal her blind when it was obvious he had more than enough wealth to sustain him.

"I built it a few years ago when the construction business was in a slump."

"Before you got out of it?"

He nodded. "Instead of laying off the men, I kept them busy here for a couple of months until business picked up. Then I sold out altogether." He pulled a deck chair around to face her and sat down, lifting his feet to rest on the stone wall beside her.

Carlson wouldn't discover anything different from what she already knew, Mallory realized. Two nights earlier, Jake had asked her to trust him, and she'd said she would try.

The previous night, she'd known it wasn't any longer a question of trying. She loved him . . . trusted him. She wanted him to know that she'd believed in him before she saw his house, this luxurious symbol of what he'd done with his life.

But first she needed to tell him why it had been an issue in the first place.

"There was something I meant to tell you last night, but I guess I was too tired," she said, blushing when she remembered how she'd fallen asleep and all that had gone before.

"I remember," he said. Clasping his hands behind his

head, he relaxed and watched the sky's natural light reflect in her hair. She was so much the woman he'd always wanted, he realized. He loved her without knowing why, but it didn't matter, not knowing why.

The thing she needed to tell him was also unimportant, he thought, because nothing was more vital or alive than the way she made his heart pound with just a look, a touch. Did she feel the same about him? he wondered. He had to believe she did, because such deep, wide-ranging emotions couldn't have evolved from a one-sided attraction.

He waited for her to speak, knowing that when she was done, he would take her in his arms and erase the worry from her heart. He'd love her slowly tonight, he decided, with finesse instead of urgency.

"I told you before that I thought you were after my money," she began, avoiding his eyes.

"I think I got the gist of that the other night," he said. "I've thought about it a lot since then, and I have to believe there's a precedent for what you imagined."

"There is." She breathed more easily, glad he'd purposely given her an opening that made her explanation sound quite rational. "My sister fell for a con artist who swindled her out of the trust fund Mom left her and then married her so he could have a try at Dad's money too."

"Your father has a lot?" Jake asked as though he were showing polite interest.

Mallory nodded, swallowing hard as her gaze glanced over his expression, and she saw an impassivity that wasn't nearly as reassuring as his unemotional questions. "That's why Carlson lives with me, you see. When I decided to move out here, Dad said it was either him or Aunt Agatha, and I really didn't want to live with her." Then Mallory told him the story from the beginning, how badly Norman had hurt not only Meredith, but the whole family.

"So Carlson is kind of a baby-sitter," he said.

"I call him my keeper. He keeps me out of trouble. Well, most of the time," she added, remembering her impromptu striptease at Jake's restaurant. "And he keeps me company. Mostly, though, he's supposed to keep me away from men who might be after my money."

"And the thought of you and Carlson living together doesn't bother your dad?"

"Heavens no!" she exclaimed, ridiculing the idea with a little laugh. "Carlson used to be Dad's chief of security. He quit to do something else and I kind of offered him a place to live while he sorted out the other thing."

"What other thing?"

"That's Carlson's secret."

Jake let that one go by because it had nothing to do with him. He dropped his feet to the flagstones and leaned forward, resting his forearms on his knees as he considered the woman in front of him. He'd guessed most of what she'd said, but there were some things she'd left out that mattered more than all the rest of it put together.

"Mallory?" he said softly. He waited until her gaze met his own, because he knew her eyes would give him the answer before her mouth could form the words. "How do you know I'm not?"

"Not what?"

"Not after your money. How do you know this house isn't a front, that it doesn't belong to a friend who lent it to me for the evening so I could mislead you?"

The night took on an uneasy silence as Mallory shuttered her eyes from Jake. He waited, though, without moving, not wanting to distract her. This was possibly the most important thing he would ever ask of her.

If she knew the answer to this, nothing could come between them.

"Because I trust you," she said quietly, lifting her lashes to return his gaze. It was what she'd been wanting to tell him since yesterday, when she realized that she loved him and, with that, assumed he would never hurt her.

Jake could have sworn his heart stopped as he looked into her eyes and saw the truth in them. Even with only the stars and the moon for light, he knew what he saw couldn't be a lie. She trusted him without reservation.

Leaning forward, he took her hands in his, threading his fingers with hers. It felt as though it were the first time they'd touched. Smiling gently at her, he slowly rose from the chair and pulled her from the wall.

"Thank you," he said simply, and pressed his lips to her forehead.

Mallory stepped closer, tilting her chin so that his mouth fell onto her lips. She reveled in the knowledge that she'd pleased him with her words. In loving him she'd discovered a capacity for trust that hadn't been there before Jake.

"I've never made love to you in a bed," he said seductively, dragging his mouth across her cheeks and nibbling on her ear.

"We're not in bed," she murmured.

His tongue dove wetly into her ear, and she collapsed against his chest. She kissed the skin exposed by the V-neck of his sweater, tugging with her teeth at one soft curl, then another.

"If you quit kissing me, I'll see if we can make it inside," he bargained, reluctantly pulling her to his side so that he could walk. With his arm around her shoulders, he led her toward the door.

"I wasn't kissing you," she corrected him. "I was merely tasting your chest."

Jake groaned and wrenched open the door.

They hadn't turned on any of the lights on their

earlier passage through the house, so Jake didn't see the smile on her face. Instead, he heard the teasing laughter in her voice and found himself totally distracted by it. Negotiating the hallway with the aid of moonlight and habit, he could feel the excitement growing inside him.

Mallory stumbled over the first step at the bottom of the staircase, and suddenly found herself aloft in Jake's arms. "Being klutzy has its own set of advantages," she said, twining her arms around his neck as he proceeded up the stairs.

"Any excuse would have done," he said. "I like carrying you."

"I have to confess it makes me feel all tingly inside." She traced the outer shell of his ear with her tongue and felt him stiffen, the hard bands of his arms tightening around her. It was electrifying, she thought. This thing between them took so little to ignite—a lick here, a taste there.

And it was gratifying to know Jake was as affected as she.

"Do that again and you'll have carpet burns on your butt," he growled, ducking away as her breath tickled his damp ear. There was only so much he could take, and her tongue pushed him to a limit he wasn't ready to reach.

He had promised himself slow. Slow, sweet, and very, very hot. Suddenly, a vivid picture of her flickered across his mind—*Mallory, gloriously naked, lying upon his pillows, her eyes half closed, her lips parted as she held his head to her breast, watching his mouth move up the gentle curve toward the taut peak.*

He gazed at her face as her eyes drifted closed, leaving her other senses to deal with his own brand of erotic torture. When his tongue began to draw circles around the dark aureole, he felt her breath quicken. When his teeth closed gently a—

"Jake?"

He heard her as though from a long distance. Shuddering at the intensity of his fantasy, he looked down to find her still in his arms. "You called?" he managed to choke out.

"I think you went somewhere without me," she murmured. "Want to tell me about it?"

Excitement shot through every nerve in her body at the look he gave her, making her forget his pause in the middle of the staircase. Anticipation was everything now, and she held his smoldering gaze as he resumed his climb.

"I'll tell you about it later," he promised. He reached the top of the stairs and turned left into an open doorway. "In the meantime, I've got other plans."

"As long as they include me . . ."

He didn't loosen his hold on her, just changed it. One moment, her feet were in the air. The next, she was sliding down his body, testing his hard frame with her softer curves. When her feet touched the ground, her mouth was open under his.

It was fleeting, though, his wet and exciting kiss. She protested when he drew back, almost reeling at the sudden void of sensation.

"I'm going to turn on the light," he said.

He wasn't asking if she minded, she realized breathlessly. He was telling her. Drawing the tip of her tongue across her swollen lips, she saw him move through the shadows, reaching out to flick a switch.

Suddenly, in the soft light of the bedside lamp, she could see the passion in his eyes. He showed her his hunger and read her own. She swayed, light-headed with the emotions that were running rampant through her body.

"My mother warned me about women like you," he said as he closed the distance between them. Looking into her face, he wondered how he'd ever imagined he could take her slowly when all he wanted was to be inside her before he burst with needing her.

"She did, did she?"

A chuckle escaped her lips, the sound low and lusty to his ears. He stroked a trembling hand down her back, followed the luscious curve of her fanny with interest. "She said women like you would take advantage of me if I wasn't careful."

"You think I'll take advantage of you?" she purred, sucking in a deep breath as his hand firmed against her bottom, rimming the seam of the slacks that ran between her buttocks.

"I certainly hope so," he answered.

He leaned down to kiss her. Mallory submitted to his caress for a second, no more. Then, when she figured Jake was as much off guard as she could expect him to get, she pushed him down onto the bed and proceeded to take advantage of him.

Later that night, with his chest still heaving from the effort to breathe, Jake wondered what other adages his mother had quoted that might be of interest to the woman sprawled unconscious atop him.

The early morning sunlight was determinedly penetrating the curtains when the telephone rang. Jake was just stepping into the shower and he shouted for Mallory to answer it. "If it's Vincent, tell him I'll be in this afternoon and not before."

She rolled over to the other side of the bed and picked up the phone before it could ring a third time. "He'll be in this afternoon and not before," she said.

"Assuming I'm not going to argue with you about Jake's schedule," Carlson's laughing voice responded, "could you tell me instead when *you're* going to surface. Jeannette just called and said she can't get to the gallery before noon."

Mallory swung her feet to the floor and stretched with one arm as she peered through the woven drapes at what was a beautiful day. "Good morning," she said nicely, calculating what it would take to convince Carlson he needed to watch the gallery for her that morning.

"I'd say the same except I know that tone of voice," he returned swiftly.

"I'm a generous woman," she said. "If you cover for me at the gallery until Jeannette shows up, I'll take you out to dinner."

"Where?"

"Anywhere you choose." She knew it was a mistake, but she was too excited about the idea of joining Jake in the shower to bother about throwing away her negotiating position.

"Tonight?"

"Maybe," she said without any intention of doing so. She and Jake had planned to spend the coming evening in much the same way as they'd spent the last, and dinner with Carlson didn't figure into the agenda.

"Then I'll just have to make sure it's expensive when I decide to collect," he said. "In the meantime, I have that report for you about Jake."

"Too late," she said, wishing she'd thought to tell Carlson not to bother with it. She didn't need other sources to corroborate what she already knew.

"You've already told him?" he asked.

"Last night. It just seemed to be the right thing to do."

"Then you'll be glad to hear everything I discovered on my end agrees with your instincts. Jake Gallegher is not only respected in business circles, he's well liked. And from all indications, he's rich enough to keep you in the style to which you are accustomed without having to bother your dad for a single dime."

"I knew that." She laughed when Carlson grumbled something before he hung up about being unneeded, unwanted, and unappreciated. Mallory took five seconds to do a full stretch with both arms, then hurried into the bathroom because she wanted a share of the hot water before Jake used it all.

Ten

Driving with Mallory was always something of an adventure, Jake mused, and this time was no exception. Riding shotgun—as usual—on the twisted trail that led up the side of Mt. Tamalpais, he paid not so much attention to the driver as he did to the acrobatics the car was performing.

Mallory steered aggressively through a hairpin turn, and Jake felt his stomach rotate ninety degrees. His normally dark complexion took on a vaguely green hue as she powered through another curve, then whisked them down the short-lived straightaway before diving into the next bend.

The Jaguar was enjoying its morning run.

When she finally eased the car to a stop, Jake managed to keep his sigh of relief to himself as he pushed open the door and planted his feet on firm ground.

"I love coming up here, don't you?" she said. Skipping around the front of the car to join him, she grabbed his hand and pulled.

He resisted, enjoying the sensation of the simple act of standing. Dragging deep breaths of air into his lungs, he concentrated on putting the effects of the roller-coaster ride behind him. "I'm not sure I like it as much as I used to," he muttered, slipping the keys from her fingers and into his pocket.

"My driving scares you?" she asked, her face alight with glee at the prospect.

"Your driving is fine. It's the road that scares me to death."

"So maybe you should close your eyes," she suggested playfully, lifting her arms to his shoulders.

"And maybe I should let you sit in the passenger seat and give you a dose of your own medicine," he countered, dipping his head to meet her mouth. Her lips parted under his, and his tongue invaded the warm cavern, stroking, teasing.

Mallory threaded her fingers through his hair, pulling him harder against her mouth. The drive up the mountain had been exciting, but it was nothing compared to the thrill she experienced at Jake's touch. She was hungry for him, eager to relive the wondrous passion they'd shared throughout the night. She tightened her fingers in his hair as his tongue slid across hers in a rhythm she recognized. Totally dependent upon the arms that held her, she stood high on her toes, wanting more, needing it all.

It took the sound of another car pulling alongside the Jaguar to force them apart. Sharing a look of mutual frustration, they reduced the embrace to a simple twining of fingers and turned to walk up a nearby hill.

Slanting a glance at her, Jake knew he'd never seen Mallory looking more beautiful. It wasn't the stark white sundress that caught his imagination, although the way the wind billowed the skirt around her knees caused his throat to dry. And her hair, pulled back into a simple ponytail with a chartreuse ribbon—which matched the glasses she'd left in the car—wasn't the most provocative hairstyle she'd worn.

Her glowing face, totally bereft of makeup, was laughing up at him, her eyes sparkling in the morning sun.

The color of sherry, he mused, remembering how they darkened in anger, clouded in passion.

She was beautiful in a way he couldn't define. Was it because he knew he loved her that made the difference? Or could it be that Mallory herself had fallen in love? His heart skipped several beats as he contemplated the ramifications of that. Having Mallory in his life forever was suddenly a distinct possibility, and he'd never imagined a life so full of joy.

"I still won't let you drive," she said, drawing his mind back to their earlier conversation, "and using sensual blackmail won't make me change my mind."

"Does that mean I should stop trying?" he asked as they negotiated the grassy slope.

"Don't you dare!" Grinning at the wolfish look in his eyes, Mallory felt her breath quicken. It was so simple to picture the two of them, lying on a blanket of wildflowers beneath the morning sky, practicing the erotic lessons they'd so recently shared.

Swinging her to a stop in front of him, Jake cupped her face, holding her still for his lips. He kissed her lightly, his tongue only teasing. "I can see what you're thinking," he said against her mouth. "And if you don't stop looking at me that way, I won't be able to walk."

"So who wants to walk?" she breathed, stunned by the sensual throbbing that weakened her knees.

"You're the one who suggested this field trip," he reminded her, recapturing her hand before backing away. "Let's get it over with." He pulled her on toward the crest of the hill, less eager to share the beauty of the view than he was to return with her to the privacy of his home.

It suddenly occurred to him that this would be as good a place as any to propose marriage to her, and he grinned as he admitted the excursion to Mt. Tam had been one of Mallory's better ideas.

He set his thoughts to putting the right words together, needing to make it as clear as possible that he loved her, wanted to marry her . . . and didn't intend to take no for an answer.

Mallory snuck a peek at Jake, wondering what had brought on his sudden smile. But then, her own mood was almost jubilant as she mixed in her thoughts memories of the previous night with dreams of tomorrow.

Permanency, the future, and sharing it with the man she loved had never been such a reality before now. She'd been too busy being defensive to get involved, paranoid because of Meredith and Norman. But now, with Jake, it all seemed so natural.

That was why she'd brought him up to the mountain.

She loved Jake and she wanted to tell him in the open, fully clothed, not in the aftermath of lovemaking. She needed to make him understand that passion hadn't brought the words to her lips.

"We should have brought a blanket."

His words startled her out of her thoughts, grabbing her interest as she let herself be distracted by the warmth in his eyes that told her he was happy to be with her.

"Why a blanket?" she asked.

"Because it would be nice to sit here and enjoy the view, maybe talk a little." *Or maybe I'll just propose,* he finished silently. He took a couple of deep breaths because he was about ready to do it and he was more nervous than he'd ever imagined possible.

"We can get by without a blanket," she said knowingly. "Trust me."

Talk a little, he'd said. Mallory couldn't help it as her thoughts returned to the long night before. They'd talked then, too, and it had been a different kind of bonding, but one that was equally as important as the sexual attraction that had drawn them together. They had revealed secret goals and aspirations, compared their minute likes and dislikes, good habits and bad.

She had discovered that Jake was not only a man she loved, but one she respected. Without reservation, without question. He was a man she wanted to spend her entire life loving.

They hadn't said the words, hadn't said *love* at all. But then, some things didn't need words, not right away.

She could *feel* his love.

It gave her the courage to decide to tell him first. And she would, soon. Before she lost her nerve.

The cushion of flowers and grass where they finally settled was wonderfully soft, and Mallory sighed in contentment. It was almost heaven, sitting beside Jake, his arm around her shoulders, the view of the distant bay enhanced by the glorious scent of wildflowers.

"I wish I'd known when I met you that it was going to turn out this way," she said, her lips brushing his cheek before she tucked her head against his shoulder.

"It's been less than a week," he said. "I'm not sure that counts as wasted time."

"I guess with all those stupid secrets between us, five days is doing pretty well." Shifting closer to his warm embrace, she sighed in happy reflection.

"I didn't have any secrets," Jake said.

"Yes, you did. All that stuff about your investment company wouldn't have made me so paranoid if you'd been up front about it."

"It certainly wasn't intentional. I was trying to be discreet for business reasons. And I wouldn't have said anything about it at all if you hadn't tried to pry it out of me."

"Who needed to pry with Harry around?" she teased. "Added to the way Carlson was dragging his heels, I guess it could have been worse."

Jake smiled down at her, a little confused but getting

used to it. "What does Carlson have to do with anything?" It seemed like he'd asked that question a lot lately.

Contented and relaxed, Mallory yawned. The lack of sleep was beginning to make itself felt. "The background check he ran on you," she said casually. "If he'd done it right away, I would have known better than to suspect you and Harry of trying to scam me."

"Background check?"

"Um-hmm," she purred, her limp body taking note of the sudden tension in his but ignoring it.

"You had Carlson check me out?"

"Of course." She turned in his arms to look at him. "That's part of his job."

Too late, she saw the fire. It wasn't an expression of desire, she realized, noticing his clenched jaw, feeling the rigid muscles of his arms across her back. She knew what his eyes looked like in passion, and this wasn't it.

This was anger.

When he saw her puzzled gaze, the flames turned to ice, and anger became rage. The next words out of his mouth were coldly delivered, ensuring her understanding the depth of his fury.

"You had me investigated to find out if I was rich enough to suit you." It wasn't a question. It was a statement.

"You're deliberately misunderstanding me," she said. "Carlson just made sure you weren't after me for my money." And that, she hoped, was plain enough for anyone to see.

"And if I'd been poor, that would have been the end of it," he said flatly. "You'd have retreated behind your baby-sitter's defenses rather than get involved with a man who couldn't buy you."

His arms dropped away from her, leaving her strangely cold in the brilliant sunshine. Mallory trembled, suddenly afraid she'd made a mess she couldn't fix. He was upset at being investigated, but there was nothing she could do to change that.

Still, she had to try. "It was nothing personal—"

"*Nothing personal!*" he thundered. "Having someone snoop through your bank balance isn't *personal*?" He rolled to his feet and dusted off his slacks with quick, hard swipes, berating himself for trusting her in the first place and feeling so incredibly stupid. He'd assumed from the beginning that Mallory didn't care about his money. "I thought what we had between us was just that—between *us*! But you can't seem to keep Carlson out of the picture, can you?"

"I told you about my sister!" she shouted back, feeding off his anger as she rose from the bed of flowers and grass. "You know why this was necessary!"

"I know only you're a spoiled little girl that has to look to her keeper for all her decisions," he spat out, clenching his fists at his sides. "No wonder there wasn't another man in the picture when I met you. I can't think of a self-respecting male who would put up with all the games you play!"

She could have put a stop to his accusations by telling him Carlson hadn't given her the report until just an hour or so earlier. She could have, but she didn't because she was suddenly as angry as Jake.

He had asked her for her trust, and she'd given it to him. Now, in return, he refused to do the same for her.

Seething because she wanted to hit something and Jake didn't look as though he was in the mood to duck, she gritted her teeth and said the one thing that made any sense at all. "Get out of my life, Jake Gallegher. Get out and stay out!"

"With pleasure." Throwing her a last scathing look, he swung around to head back down the hill. He took three steps, then whirled back to snag her wrist. She snatched it back and dared him to try it again.

"You can either come with me right now or I'll leave

you here," he ground out, showing her the car keys he'd pocketed. Then he recaptured her wrist and set off down the hill at a pace that forced her to trot along after him.

"You're sure as hell not driving back!" she yelled, finding anger made her feel less vulnerable than the hurt it covered.

Coming to an abrupt stop, he whirled her around to face him. "Don't offer me a challenge right now, sweet stuff. I just might take that precious car of yours and wrap it around a telephone pole."

"Over my dead body," she muttered.

"The way I feel, that could be arranged." As abruptly as he'd stopped, he turned and charged down the rest of the hill, Mallory in tow.

When they reached the car, Jake took the precaution of opening the passenger door before tossing the keys across the roof to her. No way was he going to let her maroon him on a mountain high above the bay. By the rebellious look in her eye, that was exactly what she had in mind.

He studiously ignored her as she settled the chartreuse glasses on her nose. When she carefully slipped on a pair of driving gloves she'd retrieved from under the seat, he pretended not to notice.

That was not the first mistake he'd made that day. He'd said terrible things to her, things he didn't mean. But the anger he'd loosed on the hill was no match for the appalling hurt that was tearing him apart inside. He'd allowed himself to believe that she wanted him and not his money, and he'd been fooled. Again. It was a replay of his marriage, a mistake he'd sworn never to repeat.

Mallory loved him no more than his ex-wife had. Without his money as an enticement, she wouldn't have given him the time of day.

They didn't speak again.

If Mallory had used the road coming up as a morning workout for the Jaguar, it was a punishing race on the way down. She refocused the adrenaline from their argument on the car, pushing it to its limits as she plunged down the mountain. She forgot her passenger, forgot their fight.

The hairpin curves absorbed her energy and tested her skill. Not once did the wheels fight the pavement. Never did she get the feeling she was out of control.

But to the passenger, it was harrowing ride.

Jake forced his hands to remain flat against his thighs, feigning an indifference he didn't feel. Mallory knew what she was doing; he gave her that.

She was scaring him to death.

When the brakes started smoking, she grinned and cut the silence with a silky taunt. "That happens sometimes. The brakes just burn up on this little hill."

"In England they have a traffic ticket for what they call 'very, very bad driving.'"

"I'm not driving badly." She smiled thinly. "I'm driving fast."

"You don't have to go to England to get a ticket for that," he shot back, his pounding heart settling a bit when he saw the road flatten ahead.

Mallory didn't reply. Her gaze focused on a telephone booth at the approaching crossroads. She'd leave him there, not because she wanted to, but because he would be better off. It had been a stupid thing to do, racing down the mountain like that. Not dangerous, because she knew the car and her control of it, but stupid because she'd revealed yet another childish aspect of her personality to Jake.

She needed to get him out of the car before she did something even more childish . . . like cry.

"That *damn* fool girl *damn* near got us killed!"

Jake's closing condemnation of the morning's excursion to Mt. Tamalpais differed little from his opening comments, with the possible exception that his tone was just a tad more defensive. With Vincent chuckling openly at his detailed description of the events, Jake knew his efforts to secure even a little compassion were doomed for failure.

"Your little adventure didn't seem to hurt your vocabulary," Vincent said, choking back another laugh. "It may be a bit limited, but it seems to express the point."

"*Damn right!*" Jake whirled away from the desk, striding across the office to look out the window.

"You have to admire her, though," Vincent drawled, propping his feet on the desk as he lounged back in the leather chair behind it. "If she was trying to kill you, it doesn't appear she minded going down with you."

"And you admire her for that?" He leveled a hard stare at the other man, working hard now to maintain the level of his anger. Without it all that would be left was the emptiness.

Vincent interrupted his somber thoughts. "All I know is that her driving terrifies you. Happens to married couples all the time."

"*Married!* I wouldn't sleep in the same house as that woman, much less marry her!" Turning his back on the quiet afternoon street below, Jake concentrated on the anger.

"Or houseboat . . ." Vincent suggested.

"That either!" Jake swallowed hard to keep back the pain, because it was no longer a matter of pretending it didn't hurt. It was killing him inside, the emptiness. The only thing left was his pride, making him act a part that Vincent couldn't penetrate.

"Pity." The older man shook his head, his expression one of true lament. "I thought you two were destined to make magic together."

Deliberately ignoring Vincent's disappointment, Jake pursued the subject of the houseboat. "Not that there's room for me on that boat," he said. "With her keeper always around, I'm surprised she dates at all!"

"Keeper?"

"Carlson," Jake said evenly. "Hadn't you figured that out?"

"Guess I didn't bother to ask," Vincent replied, working hard to keep his grin to himself. "I didn't think Carlson was with you this morning," he added.

"He might as well have been. Mallory doesn't do anything without checking with him first."

"I can't figure out if you're mad at Carlson or at Mallory."

"Both!" Throwing himself into the only other chair in the room, Jake plunked his feet on the desk and leaned back to stare at the ceiling. "She won't take anyone at face value, and he panders to her."

"I don't suppose you'd admit to a slight exaggeration?"

Snorting his dissension, Jake continued his tirade. "Anyway, with the two of them putting every eligible male under a microscope, there's not a lot of room left for trust."

"They didn't pin *me* under a lens," Vincent said, sounding a little piqued at being left out.

"You aren't in love with Mallory—"

"And you are?"

Jake stared hard at the man who was sitting in what used to be his chair. "In love?" He laughed harshly, wondering what had made him make such a slip. "In love? Not if I can help it!"

"That's an iron will you've got there, lad," Vincent said, sugared admiration coating his words.

"Inherited it from my granddad."

"And here I thought you'd gotten it out of one of those self-improvement books."

Jake's feet dropped to the floor as he straightened to

stare at the other man. "What are you talking about now?"

"Just saying I hadn't imagined that your stubbornness was inherited—"

"*Stubbornness?* What happened to iron will?"

Vincent smiled. "Whichever."

"I'm not being stubborn! She had Carlson investigate me—"

"Part of the routine, I gather," Vincent interrupted, leaning forward to flip pages of the desktop calendar.

"But I don't have to like it." His anger was fading, though, and Jake realized Vincent had seen through it from the beginning.

"That's up to you, of course." Vincent shrugged and studied his calendar with faked absorption. "But I think it's a minor point, considering . . ."

Considering how much he loved Mallory, Jake finished silently. But it was too late, because he'd already made a mess of things. Still, he tried once more to convince himself that his righteous indignation was justified. "If I'd been poor, things would have turned out different—"

"Seems to me," Vincent interrupted again, "either way, you're still doing without one exciting woman." Twirling Jake's gold pen between his fingers, he contemplated the other man with almost casual indifference as he delivered the blow. "Personally, I figure if you doubt that she'd love you if you were penniless, then it's your own self-esteem that's lacking. Putting the blame on Mallory and her relationship with Carlson won't make that go away."

"Don't put this on me," Jake warned, standing up in a move that was both defensive and angry. "She judged me by a set of standards that began and ended in dollar signs."

"And by your own standards, you returned the favor."

•   •   •

"Maybe I should go live with Aunt Agatha."

Plumping a cushion against the bay window, Mallory resumed her unfocused study of the water. It was quiet that day, a weekday with people at their offices instead of frolicking in their boats.

"She talks to her plants," Carlson said dryly from behind her. Lounging comfortably on the nearby sofa with both arms resting along the back, he waited for Mallory to continue.

"So what. Lots of people talk to their plants."

"But hers talk back."

"We only have her word for that," Mallory answered, determined to see the best in her father's sister.

"You want to share a house with a woman who plans her day according to a horoscope reading she got from a begonia?"

"She's harmless!" Peeved that Carlson was parroting her own arguments against living with the eccentric woman, Mallory turned her back on the window and leaned against the cushion, arms folded defensively across her chest.

"And you're running away."

It wasn't said as a reprimand, but rather as a statement of fact. Mallory mentally flinched and tried to keep her voice indifferent and emotionless. "Why should I run away? Jake has no interest in ever seeing me again. It's just that living with Aunt Agatha sounds appealing right now."

"I'll tell your dad you said that," Carlson said, then went to the crux of the matter. "And besides, it was just a fight."

"He called me a spoiled little girl!" Chin trembling at the insult, Mallory fought back the tears that had threatened all day.

"You're not spoiled?"

The rebuke was delivered with a gentle smile, and she lost the incentive to argue with Carlson. "That's beside the point," she said, self-consciously plucking at the lace on her blouse. "And I happen to think *spoiled* is a bit harsh."

Carlson compromised by a degree or so. "I guess we can all admit to being a bit self-indulgent on occasion."

"Thank you." Nodding regally at his concession, she was unprepared for the aftershock.

"You're just more self-indulgent than most," he said fairly, eyebrows raised as though daring her to quibble. "Sharing the Jaguar would go a long way toward alleviating that tendency."

Mallory was back on firm ground with that one. "Fat chance, Carlson. Besides, I'm not mad about the *spoiled* part. It's *little girl* that offends me."

"Well, perhaps he was referring to your stature."

Her expression instantly changed from offense to disdain. "Five foot six isn't little."

"If you say so—"

"And I'm not a girl. I'm a woman."

"I think he knows that, Mallory," Carlson said softly.

"I thought he understood about my sister," she went on, still bewildered by Jake's insensitivity.

"Doesn't look like it."

"No, it doesn't. And I guess it's too late to do things differently." Turning to stare blankly out the window again, she was unaware of the first tears that streaked down her cheeks.

"He's not as close to what happened to Meredith as you are," Carlson reminded her. "Give him a chance."

But she denied him even that because she couldn't forget that Jake hadn't trusted her, even though he'd demanded she trust him.

"He had his chance."

Eleven

"It's been three weeks now."

Carlson and Vincent shared gloomy looks as they traipsed across the intersection and headed toward a pit stop offering water and miscellaneous other liquids. Vincent drained a paper cup and tossed it into the trash can as he waited for Carlson to finish.

"I thought for sure one of them would break before now," Carlson said, sipping his water slowly. He wanted to make sure Vincent rested a little before they continued, but the organizers were getting ready to collapse the table. Carlson and Vincent were the last of several hundred participants in the eight-kilometer walk/run race, and there wouldn't be anyone else to serve. He finished and swung back into the easy pace they'd maintained throughout the charity race. "Mallory walks out of the room every time I even mention his name," he added.

Vincent shook his head. "Jake's just as bad. I said something about the gallery yesterday and practically got cooked for it—and on my own stove!"

"Still slamming around the place?" Carlson asked, checking over his shoulder to make sure the squad car that brought up the rear was still following. It was, and he relaxed again with the knowledge that they wouldn't get run down—at least, not as long as they were still in the race.

"More like bouncing off walls," Vincent said.

"I take it you've learned to share the office, then." That had been one of the first things to happen. Jake had channeled his frustration into the restaurant, butting in on the day-to-day running and generally making everyone crazy.

"He was probably a great construction boss at one time," Vincent said, "but I fear busboys don't respond as well to his technique."

Carlson chortled, remembering an incident that had resulted in total chaos amid the luncheon crowd— something to do with Jake's idea of building a more convenient work area for the busboys. Apparently, he'd decided to use restaurant labor for the minor construction, forgetting, of course, that they weren't builders by trade. By the time noon had arrived, the dining room was aflurry with sawdust and the clamor of hammers . . . with Jake standing in the middle of it all, wondering what the hell had gone wrong.

Carlson was still laughing a few minutes later when they entered the beribboned pathway that led to the finish line. They might have been bringing up the rear, but their pride was intact because the rules said they were allowed to walk, and nowhere was it written they couldn't take their time about it.

They'd spent six of the eight kilometers thinking of ways to get even with Mallory for signing them up for the event in the first place. She hadn't come to watch because Jeannette needed the day off and she hadn't wanted to close the gallery. That was probably for the best, though, because Vincent and Carlson would have dragged her along the route by her hair if they'd seen her.

At least, that was the threat that had been mentioned

when the two men had received their pledge sheets in the mail.

After they'd considered several plans for revenge, their conversation had turned to Mallory and Jake and what should be done about them. It was obvious to even the most obtuse observer that the couple in question was entirely too stubborn for their own good.

Crossing the finish line thirty seconds behind the third to the last person, Carlson and Vincent accepted the surprisingly heartfelt congratulations of the organizer, then wandered over to a park bench beneath the shade of an enormous tree.

"I suppose *we're* going to have to do something about them." Sighing heavily, Carlson reluctantly assumed the burden of decision.

Vincent nodded in agreement. "It's the only practical solution. I can't work with Jake in the shape he's in. At least, not in any positive direction."

"And Mallory is cramping my style," Carlson said dryly. "She's crowding in on my time with Peggy."

"As in playing jealous?" Vincent asked worriedly.

Carlson shook his head, laughing. The idea of Mallory and himself was almost too absurd to imagine. She was like a sister to him, and imagining anything intimate between them was ludicrous. "Not that way," he finally said. "It's just that she's either at the gallery or at the houseboat. And when she's home, she wants company."

"And you'd like a little privacy?"

"Peggy rooms with a woman who's constantly entertaining. She tells me it has something to do with her late husband's business," he said in a tone of patent disbelief, "but I can't imagine what sort of company he ran if all he did was throw parties. Anyway," he added gloomily, "the chances for any privacy there are nonexistent."

"So we're back to the beginning. We need a plan that will get the two of them talking again."

They mulled it over for a couple of minutes, then Carlson's eyes lit up in mischievous enthusiasm. "I think I've got a decent scheme," he said slowly.

"Even an indecent scheme is worth trying," Vincent muttered, then listened carefully as Carlson outlined his plan.

It was, as Vincent had suggested, almost indecent. But it was also sensationally efficient, because not only would Jake and Mallory be forced to confront each other, Mallory would get her just rewards for making them walk eight kilometers that morning.

She'd tried to make them sweat, and, in return, would get the dunking of her life.

Jake prowled the length of his living room, hands shoved in his pockets as he waited for the doorbell to ring.

Two o'clock, Vincent had said, and Jake was still wondering why he'd insisted upon meeting at the house instead of at the restaurant. He'd tried to ask, but Vincent had raced off to prevent some catastrophe in the kitchen and couldn't be found later when Jake had gone looking for him.

Checking his watch with an irritated, jerky movement, Jake saw that it was already twenty minutes past. He considered calling the restaurant, but figured Vincent was on his way over. So he waited, pacing back and forth because he hated being there. He had only to look outside at the patio to recall in minute detail the night Mallory had given him her trust and he'd taken it.

How do you know I'm not after your money? he'd asked.

Because I trust you.

A harsh groan left his throat as he remembered. Yes, he'd taken her trust . . . and thrown it back in her face because trust wasn't something he was so terribly

good at himself. Mallory couldn't be expected to understand that, because he hadn't bothered to mention the
cold-blooded way his ex-wife had weighed his monetary
value before pretending to fall in love with him.

All Mallory had done was try to protect herself from
the same fate that had befallen her sister. It hurt his
pride that she hadn't made an exception in his case, but
then, he didn't have a sister who'd lost her heart to a
swindling Romeo.

And as long as he was being fair, Jake had to admit
that he'd taken one look at her Jaguar and gallery and
judged her a safe date.

Standing at the window and watching a small sailboat head up the channel toward him, Jake admitted
that his iron will—his *stubbornness*, as Vincent had
insisted—had crumbled just hours after she'd dumped
him at the telephone booth. In its place was an anger he
couldn't hide, a virulent self-disgust that ricocheted
against all facets of his life, driving him and everyone
around him crazy.

It was too late, he knew with a sense of utter hopelessness. Too late to change the way he'd reacted, too
late to take back the terrible things he'd said to her on
the mountain.

And it was too late to tell her he loved her, because
she'd never believe him.

Mallory ducked when the boom swept past her head,
then leaned over to trim the sail as Carlson tacked the
tiny boat across the waves. Settling back onto the
cushion, she eyed him with a serious degree of mis-
trust. "You didn't give me much warning that time."

"I tried," he lied, grinning, "but you were too wrapped
up in daydreams to notice."

"I'm not daydreaming," she insisted rebelliously. "I'm

planning what the south wall will look like if Ramón comes through with all the paintings he promised."

"No, you weren't," Carlson said. "You were thinking about Jake."

Mallory shut her eyes and counted to ten. All Carlson had done since they'd left the dock was talk about Jake and Vincent and how well the restaurant was doing until she was ready to scream at him to stop!

"You can't go on like this, you know," he continued. "If you keep trying to out-stubborn each other, you'll drive everyone around you nuts."

"I'm not being stubborn."

"Obstinate, then? Or maybe you prefer hardheaded."

"He doesn't want to see me," she ground out in a voice that almost broke because the crack in her heart widened each time she thought about it.

"At least you're not pretending you don't want to see him anymore," Carlson said quietly.

Mallory sent him a glare that bounced right back at her and made her feel worse than before. It wasn't Carlson's fault, she realized. Nor was it Jeannette's or anyone else's.

It was her own foolish pride that was keeping her from going to Jake and telling him that Carlson hadn't finished his report until after she'd given him her trust.

But she'd said the unforgivable to him, pushing him forever out of reach as her defenses had reacted wildly to his accusations. *Get out of my life, Jake Gallegher. Get out and stay out!* The words would ring in her heart always, reminding her that she'd been the one to put an end to any chance they'd had for a life together.

She swallowed and blinked rapidly to dispel the gathering tears. "I'm sorry, Carlson," she said softly. "Maybe if I get away for a while, I'll get things back into perspective. Do you think Dad would like to see me for a few weeks?"

"Not in your mood," he said shortly. "He'd just as soon shoot you as look at you."

"I thought we were talking about Dad and not Jake," she joked halfheartedly, then ducked again as the boom swung back across.

"How do you know what Jake would do if you won't talk to him?" Carlson didn't expect an answer, though, and he concentrated on steering the boat along the narrow channel, aiming for the two-storied house just fifty yards away. He turned again when he figured he was close enough, tightly this time because he wanted to get it right on the first try.

He wouldn't get a second chance, because any moment now Mallory would realize where they were.

"The sail's caught," he said, pointing to where it had snagged against the side of the boat. She raised her eyebrows as though to indicate it would fix itself if he'd steer a bit harder into the wind, but she obeyed because she was used to following his orders when he was at the helm. Standing on the cushion, she leaned forward and tugged.

Carlson took a deep breath and also leaned forward, just far enough to put his hand on her backside and shove her overboard.

"I'm going to kill you!"

"That's not a nice thing to say about someone who's doing you a favor," Carlson said in a reasonable tone as he let the sail fill. The boat moved away from the woman who was trying to swim toward it.

"Doing me a favor?" Furiously treading water, Mallory reached down to remove one of her shoes and throw it at him. It sank at least ten yards short of the target, but she tried again with the other because she was too mad to stop herself.

"Just like the favor you did signing me up for the race last weekend," he explained.

"So I apologize," she said frantically. She'd say anything to get out of the icy water. "*Come back and get me!*"

He just grinned and let up a bit on the tiller, not wanting to sail away too quickly. It wouldn't be responsible to leave her treading water without making sure rescue was imminent.

"*Carlson!*" Mallory screamed when it occurred to her that he wasn't ready to let her back on board. "*This . . . isn't . . . funny!*"

"It's not *supposed* to be funny, Mallory," he shouted back. "It's supposed to be good for you." He pointed toward the shore where Jake was running across his flagstone patio.

Mallory looked over her shoulder and recognized the man and the house and, in that brief moment, she understood her roommate's intentions. Flinging Carlson a vengeful look that left him in no doubt that he'd better watch his shadow for the next year or so, she turned onto her stomach and began the swim to shore.

Jake vaulted the low wall and skidded to a stop on the gravelly shore when he realized the person in the water was swimming toward him, apparently without any trouble. He relaxed, but wondered why the sailboat wasn't coming around to pick up the man overboard. Then he looked up and recognized the man at the stern. Carlson gave him a brief salute and levered the boat into a turn that headed him back down the channel.

Startled, Jake stared at the swimmer, who had reached the muddy banks just a few yards away. Afraid to move because he knew he was dreaming and he didn't want to break the spell, he watched as the woman he loved swam toward him.

Mallory stood up finally, stumbling a little because the mud wasn't easy to walk in and her soaked clothes weren't helping. They clung to her limbs and nearly paralyzed her movements. She slogged through the last bit of water, wondering what in the hell she was going to say to Jake. If she'd ever imagined seeing him again, it wasn't under circumstances even remotely akin to these.

Still furious at Carlson for forcing this meeting and for making her face Jake when she looked no better than a dog that had been rolling in a puddle, she stopped mutinously in about six inches of water and waited for him to acknowledge her presence.

It was a Mallory Jake had never met before.

His Mallory was designer jeans and mud and soft sweaters. She was silk and satin, fragile colors, delicate fabrics. She was bold, exotic, and so wonderfully sophisticated at times, she took his breath away.

This Mallory was dripping from her swim and filthy from stumbling in the murky shallows—and he wondered if she'd laugh when he said he recognized the mud.

She was, without a doubt, the most beautiful sight he'd ever seen.

"If you keep coming, I promise I'll never let you go again," he said softly, then held his breath. He suspected she was seriously considering returning to the water and chasing after Carlson. Anything was better than facing the man who'd crushed their dreams.

Mallory's heart nearly stopped at his words. Her gaze traveled over his spotless slacks and long-sleeved shirt, his tie fluttering in the light breeze. When she reached his face, she saw he wasn't teasing. And he didn't look at all unhappy to see her.

"You didn't let me go," she said, remembering again those terrible words that had sent him away. "I threw you out of my life."

"I don't blame you," he said. He stepped into the water and mud so that he could be near her for one last time.

He couldn't imagine she'd ever agree to forget and forgive.

Stopping just inches from where she stood, he continued. "If I could take back what I said, I'd do it in a flash. If I could trade everything I have for another chance with you, I wouldn't hesitate, not for a second."

Relief and joy and love swept through her as she suddenly realized he wanted her back. It *wasn't* too late, she rejoiced, and her heart swelled with love because she also understood he'd been hurting just as badly as she over words spoken in anger.

"It wasn't like you thought," she said quickly, seeing her chance and taking it before it was too late. "Carlson didn't tell me anything until that morning . . . and I didn't even listen then because I already knew everything I needed to know." When he didn't appear to understand, she reached up a hand that was still dripping wet and touched his lips with her fingers. "I love you, Jake," she murmured, shaking now because she was putting it on the line and there was nowhere to fall if it didn't work.

She waited, her fingers on his mouth, watching for some sign that would pull her from the edge and make her a whole person once again. But he looked away and didn't say a single word. Within moments she knew she'd tried and lost, and almost cried as the tendrils of complete devastation reached out for her.

That was until his lips parted and his tongue slipped out to caress her fingers.

He looked at her then, his eyes blazing with such fierce joy that she knew she'd won. Uncaring that she was a sodden, bedraggled mess, she threw her arms around his neck and plastered herself against him, crying out in sheer ecstasy when she felt him circle her waist in a hold that was strong and sure and so very, very welcome.

He nuzzled her throat, pushing until her mouth was

beneath his, then he took her lips in a kiss that shattered whatever was left of conscious thought. Much later, when it occurred to him that there was a perfectly good bed going to waste upstairs as they stood in the cold waters of the channel, he lifted her into his arms and waded through the muck.

He stayed with her in the shower because to let her go even for a moment was inconceivable. He peeled the clammy garments from her body, and joined in her laughter when the zipper of his trousers stuck and she had to help him. They threw everything into the corner and stood together under the streaming water, learning again the pleasures of kissing.

In the end, though, he had to rush her, taking it upon himself to wash her hair before the hot water ran out.

Mallory made a token effort of drying herself, but she gave up because Jake didn't bother at all before he lifted her into his arms and carried her to his bed.

Her hair was wet, but she didn't care. They were upside down on the bed and her feet were on the pillows, but it didn't make any difference. She was above him, her hair leaving moist paths across his chest as she reacquainted herself with the thrum of his heartbeat beneath her lips.

His hands glided across her shoulders and swooped down to cover her breasts. She half shut her eyes when he began a slow, firm massage, then felt the world spin as he twisted until she was beneath him. Her breathing shallow through parted lips, she held his head to her breast, watching as his mouth moved up the gentle curve toward the taut peak.

Jake rejoiced in the power of his masculinity when her eyes fluttered shut as his tongue began to draw circles around the dark aureole. He felt her breath quicken, and when his teeth closed around the erect nipple, her hips thrust reflexively against his.

His mouth left her breast, and his palm soothed where his teeth had tormented. She cried out, telling him to do it again, and he smiled and waited a long moment before complying.

She begged for his touch where she was hot and wet and wanting, and moaned when his fingers sifted through the curls at the base of her belly, only to retreat to the safety of her hip.

She was going mad with wanting him, but he refused to be rushed. She tried, though, stroking her fingernails across his back hard enough to get his attention, then digging them into the lean muscles lower down in an effort to bring him into a rhythm. Any rhythm would do, she fretted, but was thwarted when his hands captured hers and drew them aside.

The beginning of the end was upon them, Jake realized with a tinge of regret, because making love to Mallory was something he never wanted to stop. Threading his fingers into hers, he kissed her briefly, then waited above her until she opened her eyes to him, their brown depths a passionate whirlpool that tugged at his senses.

"Tell me again that you love me," he demanded softly, edging one knee between her legs, then the other. Spreading her open beneath him, he waited with little patience. He wanted to hear the words as much as he needed to be inside her.

Mallory felt her breath wedge in her throat as she looked up at the man she'd spent her whole life waiting for. He hadn't said he loved her, but it didn't matter. She only wanted to give him what he wanted, because she loved him too much to deny him anything.

"I love you."

"You're sure?" he asked, groaning as she lifted her hips against his in a silent plea.

"I'm quite sure," she breathed. "But I'm convinced I won't like you very much if you keep stalling."

"I'm not stalling," he said with a grin. "I just wanted to hear you say it again before I did."

"Before you did what?"

"Told you I love you, of course." He groaned with the effort it took to voice the words because she wrapped her legs around his waist and forced the union he'd been withholding . . . proving yet again that once Mallory got it into her head to do something, there was no stopping her.

Mallory rolled over when Jake emerged from the bathroom. "Leave any hot water for me?"

"A little." He crossed to the table where he'd left the pot of coffee and refilled his cup. Then he tugged the towel from his hips. Mallory had to take a deep breath as he stretched with one arm, his golden body a glorious study of sinew and strength.

She shivered a little, wanting now to touch what her eyes caressed . . . and he grinned at her because he knew what she was thinking. She thought he was coming back to do just that, to touch and be touched, but he settled at the opposite end of the bed from her, sipping his coffee as his gaze drifted over her half-naked form. She flushed, a little uncomfortable under his deliberately provocative stare, and a lot frustrated because he kept himself out of reach.

"Do you think Carlson will get lonely when you move in with me?" he asked, his heart in his throat. Even though he knew she'd say yes to the real question underlying his words, he'd learned never to take joy for granted.

Suddenly Mallory was glad there were several feet between them. "If that wasn't a marriage proposal, I think I'll break your nose," she said softly, bunching the sheet at her breasts as she rose to kneel on the mattress.

"It is, more or less," he said mildly, pretending to ignore her delightfully aggressive position. "It's a matter of protocol, though. I'm not sure I shouldn't ask your keeper first, so I thought, for now, I'd keep our discussion on the informal side."

"You're treading on thin ice, buster." Eyes glinting, she inched her way toward him until their mouths were within kissing distance. "If you think I'm going to go through Carlson on this, then you're very much mistaken."

"You don't listen to him anymore?" he teased, tossing the empty cup on the floor and grasping a handful of the sheet that she held as a shield between them.

"I stopped listening to him shortly after I met you," she said softly. "I love you, and I'm going to marry you whether you like it or not. And soon," she added with a smile.

"There's a reason to hurry?" Jake liked that, the idea of getting married soon. Pulling firmly on the sheet, he bared her breasts and leaned forward enough to feel the hardened nipples thrust against his chest. The erotic sensation made him a little crazy.

Mallory gulped and tried to remember what she meant to say. "There are three reasons to hurry," she said, "beginning with my dad. He's the one who thinks Carlson is a terrific roommate. As soon as he discovers I'm living with another man—"

"Carlson's going to tell him, do you think?" Jake asked dubiously as he ran his fingers lightly up her spine.

"Of course not," she said. She hung on to his shoulders as he toyed with the sensitive nerve endings he'd discovered in the small of her back. "*I'll* tell him."

Jake grinned and dropped a kiss on her lips to show her he fully approved.

"There another reason to hurry," she murmured.

"What's that?" he asked, lowering his head to her breasts.

She liked what he was doing, so much that her words sounded a bit strangled. "Aunt Agatha. She'll ask her begonia to chart our horoscope, and if our stars aren't properly crossed or aligned or whatever, she'll try to stop us."

"Sounds serious," he said, his shoulders shaking with laughter as he was diverted from what he was doing. Rolling onto the bed and taking Mallory with him, he covered her face with kisses, then said seriously, "I never allow talking begonias to get in my way."

Mallory smiled into his smoky gray eyes and remembered the third reason for rushing the nuptials. "If you don't marry me in a hurry, I just might let Carlson break your toes."

"He wouldn't."

"It's what he's trained for," she replied, her breath coming unevenly now because his gaze had changed from teasing to sexy, and she knew what would happen if she didn't slide out from under him right then and make a break for the bathroom.

She stayed where she was, though, because it was precisely where she wanted to be.

"I guess we'll just have to get married right away, then," he drawled, quite pleased with himself because things had ended up just where he wanted them.

"I rather thought you'd see it my way," she said.

His lips covered hers, sealing the bargain of a lifetime.

Later that night, when the moon was high and the stars were sparkling their approval at all that had transpired, Mallory and Jake set off to share the good news with the two men who were bound to want credit for a big part of it. They found them at the gallery, sitting on one of the sofas and already toasting each other with champagne.

"Celebrating something?" Mallory asked sweetly as she led Jake to the opposite sofa.

"Besides your reconciliation, you mean?" Carlson asked as he filled a couple of glasses for the newcomers.

"You're pretty confident," Mallory said. She leveled a threatening stare at the two men because she wanted them to know they weren't getting off scot-free. She'd get even, although it wasn't a priority at the moment. Jake was her priority, and she snuggled closer to him, loving the way his arm tried to pull her even tighter against his body.

"Hard to miss with a combination like you two," Vincent said. "The only difficulty was getting you in the same place at the same time."

"I nearly drowned," Mallory said.

"That was the tricky part," Carlson agreed, his smile belying any concern. "But you didn't, so unless you catch pneumonia, I'd say it worked."

Neither Jake nor Mallory said a word.

"It did work, didn't it?" Vincent asked.

"It worked," Jake said briefly, refusing to be drawn into another conversation about marriage. The one he'd had with Mallory was enough said. Now he just wanted to do it, preferably without waiting more than a couple of days.

"So I guess we're celebrating that too," Carlson said, smiling his approval at the couple.

"There's something more?" Jake asked.

Vincent smiled broadly. "Carlson sold the book."

"What book?" Jake asked.

"You sold it?" Mallory said at the same moment.

"I sold it," Carlson confirmed, satisfaction written all over his face.

"To the author!" Vincent toasted as he lifted his glass.

"When did you hear?" Mallory asked excitedly.

"What did you hear?" Jake asked with a totally confused expression on his face, joining in the toast although he hadn't a clue what they were celebrating.

"This afternoon," Carlson said. "They left a message on the machine."

"Hell of a way to learn you're going to be famous," Vincent said.

"That's marvelous!" Mallory exclaimed, leaning across the low table to hug her roommate.

"What are we talking about?"

"Carlson's book, of course," Vincent said as though he thought Jake was a little slow. "He sold it."

"You really wrote a book?" he asked Carlson. He didn't expect an answer, though, since no one had paid the least attention to any of his questions thus far.

"Have you told Peggy she's dating a romance novelist?" Mallory asked.

"You wrote a romance?" Jake said. Carlson? A romance? Jake sighed in total bewilderment, then chastised himself for stereotyping. Since it appeared Carlson had indeed produced a manuscript of some sort, he'd immediately imagined it to be a spy story, or at least a mystery. But a romance . . .

Jake chalked it up to "life's little surprises" and joined in the barrage of questions. "What do you know about romance?"

"At least as much as you do," Carlson shot back without skipping a beat.

"Do we all get autographed copies?"

"I'll sign it if you'll buy it."

"What does Peggy have to say?" Mallory asked, mischief in her eyes.

Carlson just smiled.

"Does it have sex in it?" Vincent looked hopeful, then laughed when Carlson turned a shade of deep red.

"You shouldn't be embarrassed about being a success," Jake told him.

"I'm not exactly embarrassed." Carlson hesitated for a moment, looking for the right words. "It's just that I'm a little uncomfortable—"

"And defensive," Mallory inserted.

"And defensive about people I know reading some of the, er—"

"Hot stuff?" Mallory asked with a straight face.

"Precisely."

"I guess that pretty much answers my question about sex," Vincent said, and winked at Mallory in the laughter that followed.

"Can't think why you should care one way or the other what people think," Jake said. "At best, they will admire your . . . imagination."

"And at worst?" Mallory couldn't help asking.

"They'll be asking for your advice!"

"How do you feel about walking to the restaurant?" Jake asked sometime later as he helped Mallory lock up the gallery. They'd agreed to move the combined celebration party over to where there was food and more champagne, and, not incidentally, where Peggy had agreed to meet Carlson for dinner. The two other men had already left, graciously letting Jake and Mallory know they had thirty minutes of privacy before they were expected to show their faces.

"Why should we walk when we've got a perfectly good car sitting in the parking lot out back?" she asked. She stopped to look at the man leaning against the wall, wondering what she'd ever done to deserve someone so wonderful to love.

"Because it's a nice night out," he said reasonably, "and the exercise might do us good."

"It's only ten minutes from here. We got more exercise than that this afternoon."

"You're talking about your swim?" he asked innocently, knowing perfectly well to what she was referring, but wanting to hear her say the words.

"That too," she said, grinning because it was so much fun to tease Jake. "But I think I'd rather drive all the same, because we'll need the car to go home."

"Do you have any idea how much I love you?" he asked softly.

"I think so," she said, remaining beside the desk, because sometimes it's best to keep a distance or else the words get lost in the passion. She wanted so much to hear more.

"And know that I trust you with all that I have," he said, "all that I am?"

"Yes." Her emotions rose. He was offering her his heart and his soul.

"Do you trust me, darling?" he asked.

"Yes." Completely, totally, without reservation. "Yes," she repeated.

"In all ways?" Seeing her confused expression, he elaborated. "With your heart?"

"Yes."

"With your life?"

"Of course." She smiled, thinking how meaningless life would be without him.

"With everything you are?"

She hesitated then, only because she wasn't sure she understood where he was headed with this. Still, her answer would be the same, regardless of his goal. "I trust you," she said, reveling in the freedom that trust was giving her.

Jake paused for a second before asking the final question. "And do you trust me with everything you have?"

"That seems a little insignificant against everything else," she teased.

"But no less important," he argued, waiting eagerly for her response.

"I trust you with anything and everything I have," she said easily, knowing the shadow of her sister's misfortune had finally disappeared.

Jake let his pent-up breath escape slowly, understanding that the gift of trust was the most important thing they would ever share. And because trust begat love, they had everything they would ever need.

"And if I say I believe you," he asked, "will you never again bring up the subject?" This was, in his mind, a critical point, mostly because he was about to give her a one-time-only test.

With a lightness in her heart that celebrated the resolution of her last worry, Mallory smiled in total agreement. "I promise."

"Then let's go celebrate."

She nodded, suddenly finding it hard to speak. He hadn't moved toward her, hadn't touched her. But the message in his eyes was hot and exciting and so very loving, she knew he returned her emotions one for one.

"I'll meet you outside," he said.

Thinking he needed a moment alone to absorb the enormity of the pledges they'd made to each other, she didn't argue. She took her time closing the gallery, musing that they needed moments apart just as much as they delighted in their time together. She felt breathlessly peaceful, almost as though she'd been caught up in a whirlwind and was only then getting her feet back under her.

Jake loved her. She smiled, having no doubts on that score. And he believed she loved him.

Everything in her world was perfect, she judged, reaching the counter where she'd left her car keys. They weren't there, and she realized Jake must have decided to wait in the car. Setting the alarm, she pulled the back door closed and pushed the key into the deadbolt.

The powerful roar of the Jaguar's engine abruptly grabbed her attention. She looked up in time to see the tail end of her beloved car disappear around the corner.

And do you trust me with everything you have? he'd asked just five minutes before, and she'd said yes because denying him had never crossed her mind.

Until now.

"Not my car!"

THE EDITOR'S CORNER

And what is so rare as a day in June?
Then, if ever, come perfect days . . .

With apologies to James Russell Lowell I believe we can add *and perfect reading, too,* from LOVESWEPT and FANFARE . . .

As fresh and beautiful as the rose in its title SAN ANTONIO ROSE, LOVESWEPT #474, by Fran Baker is a thrilling way to start your romance reading next month. Rafe Martinez betrayed Jeannie Crane, but her desire still burned for the only man she'd ever loved, the only man who'd ever made love to her. Rafe was back and admitting to her that her own father had driven him away. When he learned her secret, Rafe had a sure-fire way to get revenge . . . but would he? And could Jeannie ever find a way to tame the maverick who still drove her wild with ecstasy? This unforgettable love story will leave you breathless. . . .

Perfect in its powerful emotion is TOUGH GUY, SAVVY LADY, LOVESWEPT #475, by Charlotte Hughes. Charlotte tells a marvelous story of overwhelming love and stunning self-discovery in this tale of beautiful Honey Buchannan and Lucas McKay. Lucas smothered her with his love, sweetly dominating her life—and when she leaves he is distraught, but determined to win her back. Lucas has always hidden his own fears—he's a man who has pulled himself up by his boot straps to gain fortune and position—but to recapture the woman who is his life, he is going to have to change. TOUGH GUY, SAVVY LADY will touch you deeply . . . and joyfully.

Little could be so rare as being trapped IN A GOLDEN WEB, Courtney Henke's LOVESWEPT #476. Heroine Elizabeth Hammer is desperate! Framed for a crime she didn't commit, she's driven to actions she never dreamed she was capable of taking. And kidnapping gorgeous hunk Dexter Wolffe and forcing him to take her to Phoenix is just the start. Dex plays along—finding the beautiful bank manager the most delectable adversary he's ever encountered. He wants to kiss her defiant mouth and make her his prisoner . . . of love. You'll thrill to the romance of these two loners on the lam in one of LOVESWEPT's most delightful offerings ever!

And a dozen American beauties to Glenna McReynolds for her fabulously inventive OUTLAW CARSON, LOVESWEPT #478. We'll wager you've never run into a hero like Kit Carson before. Heroine Kristine Richards certainly hasn't. When the elusive, legendary Kit shows up at her university, Kristine can only wonder if he's a smuggler, a scholar—or a blessing from heaven, sent to shatter her senses. Kit is shocked by Kristine . . . for he had never believed before meeting her that there was any woman on earth who could arouse in him such fierce hunger . . . or such desperate jealousy. Both are burdened with secrets and wary of each other and have a long and difficult labyrinth to struggle through. But there are glimpses ahead of a Shangri-la just for them! As dramatic and surprising as a budding rose in winter, OUTLAW CARSON will enchant you!

Welcome to Tonya Wood who makes her debut with us with a real charmer in LOVESWEPT #477, GORGEOUS. Sam Christie was just too good-looking to be real. And too talented. And women were always throwing themselves at him. Well, until Mercy Rose Sullivan appeared in his life. When Mercy rescues Sam from the elevator in their apartment building, he can't believe what an endearing gypsy she is—or that she doesn't recognize him! Mercy is as feisty as she is guileless and puts up a terrific fight against Sam's long, slow, deep kisses. His fame is driving them apart just as love is bursting into full bloom . . . and it seems that only a miracle can bring these two dreamers together, where they belong. Sheer magical romance!

What is more perfect to read about on a perfect day than a long, lean, mean deputy sheriff and a lady locksmith who's been called to free him from the bed he is handcuffed to? Nothing! So run to pick-up your copy of SILVER BRACELETS, LOVE-SWEPT #479, by Sandra Chastain. You'll laugh and cry and root for these two unlikely lovers to get together. Sarah Wilson is as tenderhearted as they come. Asa Canyon is one rough, tough hombre who has always been determined to stay free of emotional entanglements. They taste ecstasy together . . . but is Sarah brave enough to risk loving such a man? And can Asa dare to believe that a woman will always be there for him? A romance as vivid and fresh and thrilling as a crimson rose!

And don't forget FANFARE next month with its irresistible longer fiction.

First, STORM WINDS by Iris Johansen. This thrilling, sweeping novel set against the turbulent times of the French Revolution continues with stories of those whose lives are touched by the fabled Wind Dancer. Two unforgettable pairs of lovers will have you singing the praises of Iris Johansen all summer long! DREAMS TO KEEP by Nomi Berger is a powerfully moving novel of a memorable and courageous woman, a survivor of the Warsaw ghetto, who defies all odds and builds a life and a fortune in America. But she is a woman who will risk everything for revenge on the man who condemned her family . . . until a love that is larger than life itself gives her a vision of a future of which she'd never dreamed. And all you LOVESWEPT readers will know you have to be sure to get a copy of MAGIC by Tami Hoag in which the fourth of the "fearsome foursome" gets a love for all time. This utterly enchanting love story shows off the best of Tami Hoag! Remember, FANFARE signals that something great is coming. . . .

Enjoy your perfect days to come with perfect reading from LOVESWEPT and FANFARE!

With every good wish,

Carolyn Nichols

Carolyn Nichols
Editor
LOVESWEPT
Bantam Books
666 Fifth Avenue
New York, NY 10103

THE LATEST IN BOOKS AND AUDIO CASSETTES

Paperbacks

☐	28671	**NOBODY'S FAULT** Nancy Holmes	$5.95
☐	28412	**A SEASON OF SWANS** Celeste De Blasis	$5.95
☐	28354	**SEDUCTION** Amanda Quick	$4.50
☐	28594	**SURRENDER** Amanda Quick	$4.50
☐	28435	**WORLD OF DIFFERENCE** Leonia Blair	$5.95
☐	28416	**RIGHTFULLY MINE** Doris Mortman	$5.95
☐	27032	**FIRST BORN** Doris Mortman	$4.95
☐	27283	**BRAZEN VIRTUE** Nora Roberts	$4.50
☐	27891	**PEOPLE LIKE US** Dominick Dunne	$4.95
☐	27260	**WILD SWAN** Celeste De Blasis	$5.95
☐	25692	**SWAN'S CHANCE** Celeste De Blasis	$5.95
☐	27790	**A WOMAN OF SUBSTANCE** Barbara Taylor Bradford	$5.95

Audio

☐ **SEPTEMBER** by Rosamunde Pilcher
Performance by Lynn Redgrave
180 Mins. Double Cassette   45241-X $15.95

☐ **THE SHELL SEEKERS** by Rosamunde Pilcher
Performance by Lynn Redgrave
180 Mins. Double Cassette   48183-9 $14.95

☐ **COLD SASSY TREE** by Olive Ann Burns
Performance by Richard Thomas
180 Mins. Double Cassette   45166-9 $14.95

☐ **NOBODY'S FAULT** by Nancy Holmes
Performance by Geraldine James
180 Mins. Double Cassette   45250-9 $14.95

Bantam Books, Dept. FBS, 414 East Golf Road, Des Plaines, IL 60016

Please send me the items I have checked above. I am enclosing $_____
(please add $2.50 to cover postage and handling). Send check or money order,
no cash or C.O.D.s please. (Tape offer good in USA only.)

Mr/Ms _____

Address _____

City/State _____ Zip _____

Please allow four to six weeks for delivery.   FBS–1/91
Prices and availability subject to change without notice.

60 Minutes to a Better, More Beautiful You!

Now it's easier than ever to awaken your sensuality, stay slim forever—even make yourself irresistible. With Bantam's bestselling subliminal audio tapes, you're only 60 minutes away from a better, more beautiful you!

__ 45004-2	**Slim Forever**	$8.95
__ 45035-2	**Stop Smoking Forever**	$8.95
__ 45022-0	**Positively Change Your Life**	$8.95
__ 45041-7	**Stress Free Forever**	$8.95
__ 45106-5	**Get a Good Night's Sleep**	$7.95
__ 45094-8	**Improve Your Concentration**	$7.95
__ 45172-3	**Develop A Perfect Memory**	$8.95

NEW!

Handsome Book Covers Specially Designed To Fit Loveswept Books

Our new French Calf Vinyl book covers come in a set of three great colors—royal blue, scarlet red and kachina green.

Each 7" × 9½" book cover has two deep vertical pockets, a handy sewn-in bookmark, and is soil and scratch resistant.

To order your set, use the form below.